THE GOOD LAND

LOULA GRACE ERDMAN

THE GOOD LAND

DODD, MEAD & COMPANY
NEW YORK, 1960

43988
7/29/64

© by Loula Grace Erdman, 1959

No part of this book may be reproduced in any form
without permission in writing from the publisher

Library of Congress Catalog Card Number: 59-9617

Printed in the United States of America
by The Cornwall Press, Inc., Cornwall, N. Y.

Second Printing

For all the young people who have suggested that I write a book about Carolyn, but most especially for Martha

O N E

CAROLYN PIERCE, pulling the white linen cloth straight on the long dining-room table, thought that perhaps the worst problem a girl could have was for people to think she didn't have any at all.

Here she was, almost fifteen years old, which was a special and difficult age, when you couldn't ever be quite sure whether the adults in your world were going to treat you as if you were a child or a grownup. Being the baby made things worse, for although the rest of the family loved her well enough and even spoiled her, they never took her seriously. To them, she was still just little Carolyn Pierce, the youngest, who used big words and got in everyone's way, just as she had done when the family first came to the Texas Panhandle to live, almost eleven years ago.

"Put on ten plates, and a high chair for Kathleen," Mama said now, sticking her head in at the dining-room door.

"Yes—" Carolyn told her briefly.

Mama needn't have reminded her. Carolyn knew well enough how many would sit down at the table tonight— Melinda, and Dennis, her doctor husband, and their little girl Kathleen; the twins, Bert and Dick, and their wives; Katie, home only a week from East Texas, where she had finished at the Young Ladies Seminary; Mama and Papa; and Carolyn herself. For two days Mama had done nothing but cook and bake and clean, making ready for all her children to come home. Not since Melinda's wedding had there been such a general bustle about the place.

"Katie will arrange the flowers," Mama went on.

That, too, Carolyn knew. Katie was the artistic one; turn her loose with a vase and even the raggedest looking bunch of weeds and she'd come up with something pretty. She was the one who had thought of using yucca to decorate the house for Melinda's wedding—and what was yucca but something that grew wild all over the plains? The decorations had turned out to be perfectly lovely, too. Even the twins had to admit that. You'd expect that a girl like Katie wouldn't be able to cook or do a single practical thing, but Katie got along pretty well in the kitchen, too. That came, Carolyn supposed, of having kept house and minded the family when Mama went back to East Texas to take care of Grandmother, that time the old lady fell and broke her arm.

Mama came over to the table now, absently touching a fork to line it up straight. She doesn't even think I

2

can set a table right, Carolyn thought rebelliously. If Mama won't admit that I'm growing up, how can I expect the rest of the family to think I'm not a baby any more!

"And when you are finished," Mama told her, "put the cloth over the table, so it will stay nice and clean until we're ready to eat this evening."

As if I didn't know enough to put the dust cover over the table, once it's set, Carolyn fumed inwardly.

"My goodness!" Mama cried, looking out the dining-room window just in time to see a figure on horseback riding toward the corral gate. She made her way swiftly through the door leading to the kitchen, with Carolyn at her heels. Katie, who was busy arranging some flowers at the sink, dropped one of them and turned first red, then white and then red again. She just stood there, making no attempt to pick up the flower.

"It's Boy Foster," Mama said.

"Oh—" Katie's voice sounded dull and disappointed. She went on with her flower arranging, but anyone could tell her heart wasn't in the work now.

Katie had been acting strangely like this ever since she arrived home, last Monday. She watched the road and wore her second-best dresses all the time. Mama wouldn't have let Carolyn wear such nice clothes around the house when nobody was coming. But she never said a word about it to Katie.

"He doesn't want you to call him 'Boy' any more," Carolyn reminded her mother. "He's Jim Foster now. He says 'Boy' is a silly name for anyone who's practically grown and has already graduated from high school in Amarillo and has a job there."

3

She put a lot of spirit into her words; almost, it seemed, as if it were her own case she was pleading.

"Jim Foster—" Mama corrected herself. "I knew that. I had just forgotten for the minute."

Katie didn't say a word; she probably hadn't heard her sister at all. She thinks we don't know who she's expecting to ride up that lane, Carolyn thought. She thinks we haven't even guessed it's Bryan Cartwright she's wanting to come.

Through the window, they could see Jim, who had tied his horse to the corral and was making his way toward the house. He wore dark pants and boots and a faded blue shirt. His hat was pushed back on his head. He was dressed like any other homesteader boy, but still he looked different. It was partly the way he moved, with a sort of easy confidence about him. People said Jim was quite the smartest one of the Fosters and that he'd make his mark some day. He must know this, but he never let it go to his head. They said, too, that you could never tell what was going on in his mind, for he was a great one for keeping his thoughts to himself. But he must have talked in high school. He had come out at the head of his class and had given an address at the graduation exercises, so he must have told the teachers what he was thinking.

"Go and let him in when he knocks, Carolyn," Mama told her. "I want to start mixing the pie dough."

When Jim came to the outside screen door of the back porch, there was Carolyn at the kitchen door.

"Hello, Carolyn," he said. "Is your mama at home?"

"Yes," Carolyn told him.

"Come right in, Jim," Mama called to him, her tone a rebuke to Carolyn, who was standing there like a

4

dummy, not thinking to tell the visitor to step inside.

Jim opened the screen door, came across the porch and into the kitchen.

"Excuse me," Mama said, "if I keep on mixing this pie crust. You know I'm having all the children home this evening."

"Go right ahead, Mrs. Pierce," he replied easily. "How are you, Katie?"

"Fine," Katie said, although she didn't sound too sure about the matter.

"Everything all right at your place?" Mama asked.

"Oh, fine. I rode home for the week end because I could get off now, and I didn't know when I could again. Manilla was baking a cake this morning and found she was out of lemon extract, so she sent me over to borrow some—if you have it, that is."

"Of course I do," Mama assured him.

"I could have brought it out to her, if I had only known she needed some," Jim said. He seemed a little put out with himself for not thinking about it without being told and with Manilla for not looking ahead in time. Living thirty miles from town, as did the Fosters and the Pierces, made people careful to keep things on hand.

"Oh, Manilla doesn't often run out," Mama defended the absent girl. "She's really doing awfully well, managing by herself. She's young, Jim, just a year or so older than Carolyn."

And what's so awfully young about that, Carolyn thought indignantly. Manilla is not quite seventeen, and I'm a few months short of fifteen. Neither one of us is a baby.

"And she had the responsibility put on her so suddenly," Mama went on, "with Annie leaving for Austin, and your mother dying—all right there so close together. Almost before she realized it, Manilla was taking care of the family."

That was certainly true. Annie was the oldest of the Foster children and the one who had always looked after the family. Even after she married Mr. Palmer, the schoolteacher, she had lived nearby and continued to help manage the Fosters—as well as Mr. Palmer and his two children, Billy and Sue. Then Mr. Palmer was asked to teach in the University at Austin. Scarcely had he and Annie and the children gone when Mrs. Foster, who had been an invalid for several years, died. And there was Manilla, the oldest girl at home, left with the job of looking after her family.

"Oh, she gets along fine," Jim said.

"And how is Annie making out?" Mama asked, dumping the pie dough out on the board and then leaving it to wash her hands and go to the cupboard for the lemon extract.

"Fine. She was scared at first at how she would get along with all those other professors' wives, but she says she's making out all right. She decided she'd just be herself, and that seems to work."

"Of course," Mama said. "Annie's a grand person. Just being herself is all that's necessary to make people like her."

She took the large bottle and began to pour some of its contents into a smaller one. This done, she handed the small container to Jim.

"Here—" she said.

"Thank you, Mrs. Pierce," Jim replied, taking the bottle.

"You're entirely welcome," Mama assured him. "By the way, Jim, I was just going to send Carolyn out for some apples. You know that tree of early ones, by the windmill? They're getting ripe—"

"I ought to know it." He grinned at her. "I've climbed it often enough!"

"Well, you go with her and pick up some to take to Manilla. They're good for sauce or pies, now." She turned to Carolyn. "Here, take this basket."

"Thank you, Mrs. Pierce," Jim said. He reached for the basket before Carolyn could do so. Then he started toward the door, with Carolyn trailing him. Once there, he opened it and stood aside for her to pass through first, which pleased her a great deal. She moved out with great dignity, feeling like a grown young lady.

They walked along quietly to the tree. Once there, Jim bent over to pick up an apple. He polished it carefully on his sleeve and then handed it to Carolyn. She accepted it wordlessly. He selected a second one for himself, took a bite.

"Good," he said.

"Yes—"

She wasn't interested in apples now. There was something else she needed to know and here was her chance to find out.

"Jim," she began timidly, "how is it—to go to high school in Amarillo?"

"Well," he told her, "the same as it is to go to high school anywhere, I guess."

Which didn't answer her question at all.

"Is it—well, big?" She tried again.

"Gosh, yes. Those first days I got lost every time I went inside. Every room in the building is bigger than the whole schoolhouse out here. And halls—and steps—and so on! I was always taking a wrong turn."

She had her answer now, and she didn't like it one bit. If Jim Foster, smart as he was, couldn't find his way around in the building, how was she going to manage?

"Jim," she went on slowly, "I'm going to high school in Amarillo this fall. I'm going to stay with Melinda and Dennis."

Maybe he'd understand now why she needed to know all about what she could expect, once she got there.

"No you aren't," he said teasingly, "you're not old enough!"

"I'm almost fifteen," she reminded him, with as much dignity as she could muster.

"I'm going to tell you a secret," he said in a half-whisper, first looking around to be sure nobody was listening. He acted as if he had murdered several people and was just ready to confess his crime to her. "A real secret. *I'm almost nineteen.*"

Carolyn felt her face flushing. You couldn't put any dependence in grown people—not a single one of them! Here was Jim who, only a short time ago, had opened the screen door for her so politely and then had polished off an apple for her, before he so much as thought of picking out one for himself, laughing at her now, just the way the twins did. She was both angry and humiliated.

"You ought to know how I feel about going," she protested. "Nobody else here can tell me what it's like. Melinda didn't go off to school at all. She just stayed

8

here and Mama taught her everything she knew. Katie went to the Young Ladies Seminary, and, besides, she knew all about it ahead of time because Mama went there when she was a girl. Now I'm going to high school, and you're the only one I know—*the only one*—who can tell me what to expect. How big the place is and what the teachers are like, and all the rest of it. And you stand there laughing at me!" She stopped, unwilling to break down and cry, which she was really very close to doing.

"Now listen here, Carolyn." Jim spoke earnestly and soberly; she certainly couldn't complain now that he was treating her as if she were a child. "You listen to me, Carolyn. I know exactly how you feel. I was scared to death at first, but I caught on. You will, too. It won't take long—"

"But the other girls—" she wailed. Ah, that was the whole thing. How would she get along with those strange, unknown town girls! "Will they—will they like me?"

He was silent a moment. Then he went on, speaking quietly. "You heard what I told your mother about Annie, didn't you?"

"Yes—"

"All right, that's your answer. You just be yourself and you'll make out fine."

She wasn't sure that this advice was going to be sufficient to solve her problem, but she didn't want to tell him so. Anyway, he had listened to her and had really tried to be of help.

"Thanks, Jim," she said softly.

"Oh, that's all right. And now we'd better take this basket of apples back to your mother and let me get on my way."

9

It wasn't very long until Jim was riding off, a sack of apples in his hand, headed toward home. Carolyn watched him go, remembering his words. There was going to be a lot more to getting along in high school, she suspected, than just being herself. Sometimes her real self wasn't such a very nice person. She tried to remember what her two older sisters had been like when they were the age she herself was now. Melinda had been such a tomboy that nobody had expected her to do things correctly all the time. (It was amazing, though, how she had usually managed to come out all right, even when she got into the worst scrapes.) Katie, six years older than Carolyn, was so shy that everyone felt sympathy for her right away. She was also so sweet and pretty that people rushed to help her past any hard thing that might threaten her. (And yet, when you stopped to think about it, Katie could be awfully brave when she needed to be.)

I'm not as independent as Melinda and I'm not as pretty as Katie, Carolyn thought. I can get in scrapes, the same as Melinda could, and, inside myself, I sometimes feel as shy and timid as Katie. These things the family doesn't seem even to suspect. For instance, no one appears to know now that I'm scared about going to high school this fall.

By the middle of the afternoon, things were pretty well rounded up. Mama was still busy in the kitchen, but the house was clean and shining, with the vases full of flowers that Katie had arranged making the rooms even lovelier. Katie had already put on her prettiest dress, her very best Sunday one. (Carolyn thought Mama would protest, but she didn't say a word.) Katie had combed and recombed her hair half a dozen times, although, as far as Carolyn could see, it had looked perfect the first time. Curly hair was like that. Carolyn had to put hers up on papers to have any sort of a curl at all. Katie kept watching the road, as if by keeping her eyes on it she could make someone she wanted to see come riding along. Carolyn didn't have to be told that it was not Melinda and Dennis for whom she was watching.

It was getting late—after four—when Bryan Cartwright finally came. Katie turned all colors and looked ready to faint.

"It's just Bryan," Carolyn wanted to say, but some way she couldn't bring herself to tease Katie right now.

Katie started for the door, all in a rush, then seemed to think better of it. "You go, Carolyn," she begged.

So Carolyn went to the door to open it for Bryan, and there he stood, dressed in his best. He was tall and sunburned and terribly good-looking.

"Hi, Carolyn," he said, but he looked right around her until he saw Katie. "Oh, hello."

"Hello," Katie replied, prim as anything. It was Carolyn who had to urge, "Come in, Bryan."

Maybe it was a mistake, but she led the way into the parlor. With Katie that dressed up and Bryan acting like company, it seemed the right thing to do. They followed her as if they didn't know what else to do. Once inside, they sat down.

"How are you?" Bryan asked, turning to Katie.

"I'm fine," Katie told him, speaking as shyly as she would to an utter stranger.

Bryan cleared his throat. "You look fine," he said.

"I feel fine—" Katie repeated.

11

Honestly, they acted as stiff as if they were meeting for the first time! Carolyn felt she had to do something to break the stiffness, to make things easier. "Why don't you play the piano for him, Katie?" she suggested.

"Yes—do." Bryan insisted politely.

"Well—" Katie hesitated; then went over to the piano, more it seemed to have something to do than from really wanting to play. She spread her pink dotted-swiss skirts out over the piano bench. A couple of strands of hair had come loose from the knot at the back of her head and curled loosely there against the whiteness of her skin. My goodness, her skin was lovely and white, Carolyn thought —white as that jasmine flower in the picture hanging over the piano—the one Katie had painted herself.

"Katie painted that picture," Carolyn said proudly. She wanted Bryan to know how smart her sister was. Maybe he'd stop acting so stiff and standoffish then.

Bryan shifted in his chair. "It's mighty pretty," he said. He didn't sound one bit like himself. Usually Bryan could talk and carry on with the best of them, but now he didn't seem to be able to get out more than a few words at a time.

"Carolyn," Mama called from the kitchen, as if she didn't know that they had company, "don't you want to come make some lemonade?"

Carolyn caught on quick enough. Mama thought Bryan and Katie ought to be left alone. I'm just a baby sister to Mama, and I ought to clear out when my older sister's beau comes calling. I couldn't tell Mama how things really are between those two—she wouldn't believe me.

Carolyn got up and started toward the door. Bryan looked after her uneasily. Katie seemed in a downright panic; almost as if she wanted to grab her sister by the hand and hold her there.

They act afraid to be alone together, Carolyn thought. I just don't understand it.

"It's time you dressed," Mama said when Carolyn joined her, apparently forgetting all about the lemonade. "Dennis and Melinda will be here any minute now."

"All right," Carolyn agreed. She turned her head slightly, just to check whether those two in the parlor were finding their tongues, now that they were alone. But instead of voices, there was music. Katie had started to play.

She kept at it for almost an hour. Carolyn had changed her dress and helped Mama with all sorts of last-minute errands before the music stopped. And scarcely did it die down than Bryan marched out of the parlor.

"Well, good-by, Katie," he said stiffly.

Katie didn't even come to the door with him. In fact, she didn't leave the parlor until Mama cried, "There they come—there's Dennis' automobile, just coming in the drive!"

When Katie did appear, she looked as white as milk.

Mama and Carolyn, with Katie trailing behind them, went to wait beside the windmill with its morning-glory vine running halfway up the tower. The dogs set up a great barking and the horses, that had started up to the windmill to get a drink, turned and dashed off in the opposite direction, apparently fearing for their very lives. Dennis turned the automobile into the lane, stopped it beside the windmill tower. He got out, pushed his goggles up on his forehead and went around to lift out little Kathleen and then to help Melinda.

Melinda had a veil tied down over her hat, so it wouldn't blow away, and she wore a long linen duster over her dress, to keep the dust off. Anyone else would have looked like a sack in that outfit, but not Melinda. Instead, she managed to appear very stylish.

Mama swooped down on Kathleen, picking her up in her arms.

"Oh, honey!" she cried. "How are you?"

"I am very well, thank you," the child said sedately. "I am glad to be here."

At five, she was small for her age, which made her grown-up way of talking seem all the funnier.

"Now, doesn't that sound exactly like Carolyn used to?" Melinda asked with a tolerant laugh, just as if Carolyn herself weren't there listening.

I ought to be glad they think she's like me, Carolyn told herself. She is—I can see it myself. I'm really proud.

The trouble was that the family always laughed when they said Kathleen was like Carolyn, making the resemblance seem some great joke. It *was* rather funny, being an aunt when you are ten, which had been Carolyn's age when Kathleen was born. It was almost like dressing up in Mama's clothes. Everyone thought you looked cute, but all the time they knew you were just playing at being grown. Even Kathleen seemed to realize there was something different about this relationship. When she began to talk, she said, "Aunt Katie," but, from the first, she said, "Cal-lyn." Nobody ever considered that she ought to say "Aunt Carolyn." Even Carolyn herself didn't really want it; but sometimes she thought that someone—Mama or Dennis or Melinda or *someone*—should have suggested it.

14

"How was the trip?" Mama asked, after she had kissed Melinda and Dennis, too, and hustled them inside the house.

"Fine," Dennis bragged. "Took us just a little over an hour."

He was the proudest person about that automobile. Well he might be, for it was one of the first in Potter County. He could dash off in it to treat some sick person and be back home before he could have been well started on horseback. Today, he had driven out from Amarillo—thirty miles—in an hour. Carolyn could remember when the trip used to take the best part of a day. That was when the Pierces drove to town in a wagon. Now, Papa was awfully proud because his good team could pull the carriage over the same road in less than half that time. But Dennis' trip seemed like flying compared to even that.

"We would have been here sooner," Melinda said, giggling, "if we hadn't stopped to let Mr. Frazier drive his team past us. He threatened to take the buggy whip to Dennis because his horses were so scared of the automobile. But Dennis got out and helped him and smoothed him down. Oh," she exclaimed, looking around, "it's good to be here!"

Mama's face glowed, the way it always did when her children seemed happy to be home.

"You all right, Katie?" Melinda asked, turning to look keenly at her sister.

"Oh, yes," Katie answered quickly—too quickly.

Anyone looking at Katie would know she wasn't all right. Her cheeks, usually so pink, were pale now. Sometimes she looked as if she had been crying.

"She studied too hard at the Seminary," Mama put in hurriedly.

"Aren't you thinner?" Melinda asked. They loved each other very much, those two. Carolyn always told herself sturdily that they didn't really mean to shut her out. They had grown used to there being just the two of them long before Carolyn came along, and they never quite got over it.

"Oh, a little, maybe," Katie answered nervously. "But Mama's cooking will take care of that in no time."

"*Uh-mm—*" Dennis said, looking at her thoughtfully.

"Honey," Mama broke in, turning to Kathleen, "your doll is in Grandma's room. Do you want to get it?" Obviously, Mama was trying to change the subject.

"Yes, Grandma," Kathleen told her. The child started after the doll, then turned to say, "It is very nice here. I am glad we came."

"Now who does that remind you of?" Melinda asked, raising her eyebrows as she looked at Katie and Mama.

They smiled at each other, those three. They thought Kathleen sounded the way Carolyn had done at that age, but they didn't include Carolyn herself in the look they exchanged.

Supper that night was a remembering time. Bert and his wife Ellen came—Bert with his red hair refusing to stay combed, his laugh ringing out through the rooms, his mind rushing off on all sorts of things. "Now Bert," Ellen would say gently, when he got too far out of line, and, funny thing, he would settle down right away. Dick and Sally came, too. Dick had always been the quiet one in that family, but Sally was like a little busy, chirping wren.

Dennis fitted in as well as if he had belonged to the family all his life.

"How are things going in Amarillo?" Bert asked him.

"Oh, fine—you never saw anything like the way the place is growing. I can remember when there wasn't much to it. And here we are, not ten years into the new century, and we are getting a real town on our hands."

"The whole country's filling up," Bert said. "The railroads are bringing in long strings of immigrant trains, and every one of them is loaded with families taking claims. More people to take your pills, Dennis."

"The climate here is so healthy, they won't need them." Dennis laughed.

"Remember—when we got off the train in Amarillo and Papa wasn't there to meet us?" Melinda mused.

"And you let Carolyn get lost?" Bert reminded her.

"And who found her, I'd like to know?" Melinda flashed back at him. Same old Melinda—never without an answer.

That set the Pierce family off!

"Remember the night the bad men came?" Dick asked.

"And the time Melinda thought she saw Indians and scared us all to death?"

"And when she told Dennis off—wow, did she pour it on! I don't see how you ever forgave her for that, Dennis."

"And the time she thought she had rung the fire bell and ran faster than the fire horses, back to the wagon yard."

"You boys beat me there," Melinda reminded the twins calmly.

The reminiscences weren't all about Melinda, either.

"Remember when Katie cooked the beans—pans and pans of them?"

"And made us haul up all the weeds in the canyons to decorate for the wedding?"

"And the time she killed the snake? When she got through with him, he was the deadest snake that ever crawled into the Panhandle of Texas."

Carolyn listened silently to the talk, having little or nothing of her own to contribute. She might almost as well have been an in-law, like Ellen or Sally, or even little Kathleen, for all the part she could take in the reminiscences. It seemed to her that everything they remembered was something in which she hadn't really shared—she had been asleep, or with Mama and Papa, or just watching, when these things had happened. The four big ones had always been off together, having good times, getting in and out of scrapes.

"And," Dennis broke in, for he, too, had shared in many of their adventures, even helping to find Carolyn that first day, "do you remember how close Katie came to breaking up the wedding, sending me off to Mrs. Lister?"

"She had help there," Dick reminded him. "Bryan Cartwright had his finger in the pie. By the way, Katie," he went on, turning to face his sister, "where is Bryan these days? Seems like I just don't ever see him any more."

Katie, who had been laughing with the rest of them, almost like her old self, stopped suddenly at the question. She looked as if someone had struck her. Her lip trembled a little and the color left her face.

Before she could answer, Mama broke in smoothly,

"He's awfully busy, you know. It's the rush season for farmers. By the way, Melinda, Jim Foster says Annie is getting along fine in Austin."

Bryan's name didn't come up again, but even so, Carolyn knew he wasn't forgotten. She wondered if anyone else noticed that Katie didn't have anything much to say, after that.

It was late before the twins and their wives left and the rest finally settled down for the night. Carolyn fell asleep almost immediately. She didn't have any idea what time it was when something awakened her. At first she felt frightened—although of what she did not know. She was ready to call out for Katie when she realized what had brought her out of her sleep.

It was the sound of Katie, sobbing in the darkness of the night across the room in her own bed—apart and alone, divided from everyone, even from her family that always stood by each other in time of need. She was especially apart from Carolyn, who was so close she might have reached her sister's side with only a few steps. But Carolyn did not take those steps. Some instinct told her she must not let Katie know she had heard—now, or ever— or that she suspected her sister's grief had something to do with Bryan Cartwright and his visit this afternoon.

By morning, Carolyn might act like a child again but, lying there in her own bed, very still so as not to let Katie discover she was awake, she knew she was grown-up now— very grown-up, for she was listening to her sister's crying and knowing the reason for it; and also knowing that she must conceal her knowledge.

The next day, which was Sunday, was one of tremendous activity. Bert and Dick and their wives arrived early, almost as soon as breakfast was over. Of course, their farms, which joined each other, were right next to the home place. Even so, they had started early. Hardly had they arrived when Mama sent them to the ice house; she might have been ordering two small boys to do an errand, instead of married men with homes of their own. Presently they were back with blocks of ice which had been cut off the frozen pond last winter, stored in a circular hole in the ground and covered with lake hay, to keep them from melting. The twins washed these off with water at the windmill and brought them to the house.

"Now," Mama directed, "you can freeze the cream. Take turns."

Mama orders those two men around as she would children, Carolyn told herself, so why do I mind when she treats me as if I'm still a baby?

"And do we get to lick the dasher?" Bert asked.

Mama just smiled at that.

Everyone was trying to help, getting in each others' way, talking and laughing. A regular party, that was what it was. Carolyn would have enjoyed it more had she been assigned a real job. As it was, she was given vague directions to "entertain Kathleen." She loved her niece dearly, but looking after her was not real work.

"I think I would like to go see the chickens, Carolyn," Kathleen told her.

So off they went.

When they came back, Mama and Melinda were busy in the kitchen, putting the finishing touches on the dinner. The moment Carolyn and Kathleen stepped into the room, the two women stopped right in the middle of a sentence. Katie wasn't there, so Carolyn felt pretty sure that her sister had been the subject of their conversation, which concerned something neither wanted Carolyn to hear.

"Mama," Melinda changed the subject quickly. "I do declare Carolyn looks more like Grandmother every day she lives."

"Thank you," Carolyn said primly.

She knew Melinda spoke the truth. She did look like Grandmother. That didn't mean she was pretty; nobody ever said Mama's mother was that. But they did say she had "an air," and even Carolyn could see what they meant. It was the way she sat and moved and looked at people when she talked. These traits Carolyn, as yet, did not have to any extent. But she did have Grandmother's hair —straight and thick and soft—and her eyes, a color not quite brown nor yet blue. They were, actually, a sort of hazel, although that did not exactly describe them, either. And she was going to be tall, like Grandmother. Oh, she could see Melinda was right, even though her sister had said it only to change the subject.

Just then Katie slipped into the kitchen, looking quiet and pale.

"Isn't there something I can do?" she asked vaguely.

"No," Melinda told her, "we've about finished. You should have been here—I've been telling Mama all about Amarillo."

Melinda talked a great deal about Amarillo; it was her home, and she loved it. In her house she had running water and electric lights and a telephone. Here on the farm, the Pierces got their water from the well with the creaking windmill pulling it up from the ground. They had coal oil lamps—ordinary glass ones for kitchen and bedrooms, hand-painted ones for the parlor. Papa was going to get a telephone soon, but as yet they had to depend on letters or neighbors to take messages back and forth.

Oh, Amarillo was grand beyond all telling, and Carolyn would be there herself this fall. But suddenly she wanted to run back to her own room, declaring that she never meant to leave home. Never, never! She might have done it, too, had she not remembered Katie, sobbing away in secret last night. Grown people didn't cry where people could see them.

"Mama and I were just talking," Melinda said, speaking very fast. Carolyn knew that she was resuming the conversation she had dropped earlier. "Katie, I'm going to take you home to Amarillo for a visit with me."

Katie shrank back, almost as if she were frightened that Melinda would snatch her up and carry her off against her will.

"Oh, no!" she protested. "I couldn't, Melinda. I couldn't possibly. Thank you, but I couldn't—"

"I don't see why—" Melinda began, and then stopped at a faint little staying motion of Mama's head. We have tried, she seemed to say, and we have failed.

"Well—" Melinda trailed off lamely. She was not accustomed to giving up this easily.

Again, Carolyn saw Mama signaling to Melinda. So quickly it almost seemed that Mama herself had spoken the words, Melinda went on, "Carolyn, you come home with me, then. Dennis and I are going to the medical convention in Dallas in a couple of weeks and we'll want to leave Kathleen here with Mama. We can bring you both back at the same time."

She had asked Katie first, Carolyn thought, although she knew it was childish of her even to notice this.

"That way, you'll get to know the town a little before it's time for school to start—as well as some of the girls who will be in your class." Melinda reached out and took Carolyn's hand. "We'll have ourselves a time, little sister," she finished.

Oh, Melinda was the smart one! She had probably guessed the fears Carolyn had—of the strange school and the strange young people who would go there. Maybe she even sensed the hurt at being asked last.

"And besides," Melinda continued, "you can help me no end with Kathleen."

That did it. Carolyn stood straight. She looked at her mother for the permission she knew would be forthcoming.

"Go right ahead, honey," Mama urged. "We'll pack your bag this afternoon."

"Thank you, Melinda," Carolyn said. "I'd love to go."

TWO

CAROLYN STRETCHED HERSELF half-awake, expecting all
the familiar sounds which greeted her mornings—
Mama getting breakfast in the kitchen, the windmill
creaking in the breeze, water pouring into the tank from
which the stock drank, a horse neighing in the corral
when Papa came close to it. Instead, she heard a child's
voice saying, "Carolyn, it is time for you to get up."

Then she knew where she was—at Melinda's, in the
spare bedroom, and Kathleen had come in to waken her.

Carolyn jumped out of bed and ran to hug her niece
close.

"I'm up, honey," she said. "I'm up—"

"Mama said breakfast is ready," Kathleen announced.

"I'll be dressed in a jiffy," Carolyn told her.

Melinda was bustling around the kitchen when Carolyn and Kathleen walked in. She always moved swiftly, as if she had only a little time to give to any particular chore.

"Dennis has already gone," she told the late arrivals. "Your breakfast is ready. Sit down and get busy—"

Two bowls of oatmeal were on the table, two glasses of milk and two pieces of bread and butter. Baker's bread! Town bread, Papa called it. "Melinda," he would tease his daughter, "have you become a city woman so fast that you don't make your own bread any more?"

Melinda didn't mind his teasing a bit. "Why should I spend my time baking bread when the stores will sell it to me already baked?" she would reply. Personally, Carolyn was glad she felt that way. The bread was delicious—spongy, light and very different from the kind Mama made.

"Here," Melinda continued briskly, "put some plum jelly on your bread. A patient gave it to Dennis. Now Kathleen, eat your oatmeal. Don't sit there dreaming over it."

Just the way Mama used to talk to me, Carolyn thought.

"I want to get things in order this morning," Melinda declared. "There'll probably be callers this afternoon."

"Callers?" Carolyn repeated uncertainly.

"Yes—women will come to call on me. Some of them may know you are visiting me and bring their daughters who are near your age."

Carolyn's face brightened. Here was a chance to meet girls her age. She had a vision of those girls and herself, going out into the yard to play games or some such thing. But Melinda put that idea out of her sister's head right away.

"They won't stay very long," she said, "and we'll just sit around in the living room and talk." She went on to explain that it would all be very polite and proper, stylish and fine. The women who called would leave their cards, chat a while, then go on to other homes.

"At first I thought it was a terrible nuisance," Melinda admitted frankly, "but now I like it."

It didn't sound like very much fun to Carolyn. She wanted to meet girls her own age, girls who, if things went right, would be her friends when she started to school this fall. But you couldn't make friends like that—sitting up prim and proper with grown folks right at your side. What in the world did you talk about, anyway?

"You can wear your dotted swiss," Melinda told her sister. "And your yellow hair ribbons. You'll look nice."

She knows I'm a little frightened of it all, Carolyn thought. Melinda is sweet.

By two o'clock, Melinda had the house immaculate, Kathleen in bed for a nap and herself crisp and neat in a dimity dress. Carolyn, wearing the yellow dotted swiss and the hair ribbons to match, took a last look at herself. If she kept on growing, she would be taller than Melinda. Even now, she was as tall as Katie, who was on the small side. She knew she didn't look like either of her sisters. "They adopted you," the twins used to tease her. "I am *not* an adoptioned child," she would protest, almost in tears. "I look like my grandmother, so there!" My, hadn't she been the one to use big words and words out of place? No wonder they were always laughing at her. Being the youngest let her in for a lot of teasing; but it also meant she got a lot of spoiling as well, so things sort of evened up. She never used big words now. It even embarrassed her a little to think of those days when she had always reached for the biggest ones. She wondered if the family realized she did it then because she wanted them to think she was as old and as smart as they were.

"You look nice, Carolyn," Melinda said to her sister now. "Let's just sit down and wait until the callers start coming."

She went into the living room, Carolyn at her heels. Choosing a low chair, she took out her embroidery. It was the most beautiful thing Carolyn had ever seen—a dresser scarf with red roses in variegated shades, and green leaves and brown stems, natural as life. Melinda drew out a strand of red thread and put it through the needle's eye, then picked up her embroidery frame, which held her work taut and steady. She drew her needle carefully through the cloth.

"Oh, Melinda," Carolyn breathed, "that is so beautiful!"

"I'm glad you like it," Melinda said. "I don't—I do it for an exercise in patience."

Carolyn giggled a little. Melinda wasn't just joking. Even she could remember her older sister's struggles with anything that resembled sewing or fancy work.

Melinda looked up from her stitching.

"Oh, here's someone," she said. "The hack is stopping outside. It's—yes—it's Mrs. Lindley and Elizabeth."

Through the lace curtains, Carolyn could see a woman and a girl alighting from the hack. The woman spoke a few words to the driver, who nodded. Then the two guests started up the walk toward the front door. They knocked, and Melinda went to meet them.

"Why, how do you do, Mrs. Lindley," Melinda said smoothly. Mama would have been proud of her, Carolyn thought. She looked nice and she spoke naturally, like a great lady herself. Mrs. Lindley seemed very elegant in a lilac-colored dress and a hat with a plume.

Melinda ushered the two visitors into the living room.

"Mrs. Lindley," she said, "this is my sister, Carolyn Pierce. Elizabeth—this is Carolyn—"

There was a flurry of greetings; there was a bustle of finding chairs; then they all sat down. Carolyn perched on the edge of hers, as did Elizabeth.

She is the most beautiful girl I have ever seen, Carolyn thought, noting her guest's blue eyes with their unusually long lashes, her dark brown, curly hair and fair skin. Her cheeks were very pink. She wore a blue dotted-swiss dress (a great deal like my yellow one, Carolyn thought happily), a small hat and—most unbelievable—white kid gloves! These placed Elizabeth Lindley in a sphere of elegance and smartness that she, Carolyn Pierce, could never hope to attain. They seemed to proclaim the difference between Elizabeth, the young lady who lived in town, and Carolyn, the little girl from the country.

"It is so nice that you can have your sister with you," Mrs. Lindley said. "How long will she be staying?"

"A week just now," Melinda answered. "Next week end, Dr. Kennedy and I will take her back home. We are going to the medical meeting in Dallas, and my mother will keep Kathleen for us while we are gone."

"That will be lovely," Mrs. Lindley murmured.

"But Carolyn will be coming back in the fall," Melinda went on. "She is going to stay with me and go to high school."

"How nice!" Mrs. Lindley exclaimed warmly. "You and Elizabeth must plan to see each other often."

Carolyn looked at Elizabeth.

"Oh, yes," the latter said, "we must, Carolyn."

"I'd like to," Carolyn replied. She found herself speaking most formally and correctly. Something about the whole situation—perhaps it was due most of all to the white gloves her caller wore—made her control the joy she felt at Elizabeth's words. This wasn't the way she was used to visiting. At home, people came and you rushed out to meet them and there was a great deal of clatter and talk and excitement. On the farm, a visitor was an occasion. Here, the whole thing seemed dignified and quiet, almost like going to church.

"We're having very nice weather," Melinda remarked, drawing a red thread carefully through her fancy work.

"Yes—but such a lot of rain. I declare, the streets are a real loblolly. That's why I decided to hire the cab. I wouldn't want to try to get my buggy through these streets, the way they are."

"Of course," Melinda agreed.

"Is there much sickness?" Mrs. Lindley asked politely.

"No, Dennis says there isn't a great deal. But even so, he seems to be busy most of the time."

"He's an excellent doctor, and we are lucky to have him," the visitor went on. "So fortunate he has an automobile; he can cover much more territory in less time. Although, goodness knows, I'd be afraid to ride in one. Mr. Lindley talks of buying one, but I discourage him. It's not safe to drive out farther than you can walk home, if it breaks down."

"Oh, you don't need to be afraid of having to walk

back," Melinda retorted with spirit. "Dennis drives everywhere and he rarely has had trouble."

"Dr. Kennedy is smart about machinery," Mrs. Lindley said. She looked at her watch, a small gold affair suspended from the front of her dress by an enameled fleur-de-lis. "We must be going," she announced.

The two women stood up. Elizabeth and Carolyn stood, too. There was a round of polite farewells. Mrs. Lindley made her way to the door, followed by Elizabeth. There she paused beside a table on which a tray rested. In this she deposited some small calling cards. Then, repeating their good-bys, she and Elizabeth walked out.

"I'll see you," Elizabeth turned to call back in a more natural tone of voice, as she started down the porch steps.

Carolyn watched the two visitors until they got into the hack; then, she turned to inspect the cards. They had the names of the three in the family—Mr. Lindley, Mrs. Lindley and, yes, Elizabeth—on them, one card for each person. So, Carolyn thought, town girls have their own calling cards!

"Well," Melinda said, turning back to the living room once more, "I'm glad she brought Elizabeth with her."

"Oh," Carolyn cried, "she's the prettiest girl I ever saw!"

"She's pretty, all right," Melinda agreed. "And she's a nice girl, too. Now that they've been here, we'll return the call. I need to make some calls, anyway. One day this week—maybe Wednesday—I'll rent the hack and we'll start out."

"Rent the hack—" Carolyn echoed. Mrs. Lindley had used that same expression.

"Yes, it's cheaper, in the long run. The driver will take

you for twenty-five cents a call, providing you're ready when he comes. If he has to wait, he charges fifty cents. He'll take you for an entire afternoon, all over town—and wait until you've finished all your calls—for a flat rate of two dollars and fifty cents. We'll go see the Lindleys first."

"They must have a lot of money," Carolyn said. Strange, but never until right now had she thought much about money or what a difference it could make to people. This afternoon, she had looked in on a whole new way of life.

"They're comfortable, but not extremely wealthy," Melinda told her sister. "Mr. Lindley's a lawyer. It's her money, I think. She doesn't like living here very much, but he won't leave. Yes—we'll call on them, and then we'll ask Elizabeth to spend the afternoon with you before you go home."

"Well—" Carolyn hesitated. Maybe Elizabeth wouldn't want to come. Maybe she had other things to do with other girls, ones Carolyn didn't even know.

"Now, Carolyn," Melinda said briskly, "don't draw back into yourself. You don't have to act forward, but you have to go your part of the way, too. Just be yourself. You're a very nice girl, and you don't have to feel apologetic about yourself or anything else. Remember that."

Carolyn felt her cheeks begin to turn pink. It wasn't safe even to *think* a thing around Melinda! She caught on quick as anything.

Early next morning, almost as soon as Carolyn was finished with breakfast, the telephone rang. Melinda answered it, and then turned to Carolyn. "It's for you," she said.

Carolyn went over to take the receiver from her sister. She had talked over a telephone so seldom that the experience was still a wonder and delight. "Hello," she called, loud enough to be heard a block away.

"Hello." Elizabeth's voice came, soft and easy, from the other end of the line. "I wish you'd come over and see me this afternoon. Will you?"

"Oh, I'd love to," Carolyn said. This time she spoke in a natural tone of voice. "Wait until I ask my sister whether she had any other plans for me." Melinda promptly approved the idea, so Carolyn accepted the invitation happily.

"About two?" Elizabeth suggested.

"Yes," Carolyn told her. And then she remembered to say, "Thank you, Elizabeth."

Accordingly, at two o'clock, Dennis, on his way to see a patient, dropped Carolyn off at the Lindley house. Elizabeth came out to meet her visitor. This, indeed, was no formal call. Her face was eager and bright.

"I'm so glad you could come," she said.

As if I would have missed it, Carolyn thought.

"What would you like to do?" Elizabeth asked. She seemed anxious to please her guest.

"Oh—I don't know," Carolyn answered. She remembered what Melinda had told her—that Elizabeth, being an only child, spent much time with her mother and father and didn't see other young people nearly enough.

"Do you mind—I mean—would you think it awfully *babyish* to cut out paper dolls?"

"Oh," Carolyn exclaimed, "so you still cut out paper dolls, too!"

The boys were always teasing her because they said it was silly to sit there cutting those people out of the mail order catalogues. How could they understand it was a whole new world that opened up under one's scissors; like reading a book or even almost like seeing a play the young people put on at the schoolhouse. It was fun to give the different cut-outs names and plan what sort of life they had. Carolyn often hid her paper dolls when the twins were around because she didn't want to be teased. Now, here was Elizabeth, a perfectly beautiful town girl, with her own calling cards and white kid gloves, who still liked paper dolls, too. Just wait until she got home and told the twins about this!

"Yes," Elizabeth said, "I still cut out paper dolls. I hate to think of the time when I'll have to stop. I'm *so* glad you like it, too!"

A time when she'd have to stop! The future stretched out bleakly ahead of Carolyn, bringing a time when she must give up such delights. Wasn't it strange—when she was little and so far away from being grown-up that she couldn't even imagine she'd ever get there, she had tried to act grown-up; yet now, when the time seemed just around the corner of her life, she wanted to hold fast to the dear, familiar, childish things.

"We'll work out on the back porch," Elizabeth told her guest. "That way, we won't litter up the house."

Together, the girls went to the back porch, which was screened in and had a table and chairs set up. On the table were magazines, two pairs of scissors, some extra paper and a bowl of paste. Everything was immaculate and extremely orderly. In fact, Carolyn rather suspected that Mrs. Lindley would not have allowed paper cutting in that fine parlor, with its Brussels rug and lace curtains and lovely furniture; nor even perhaps in any other room in the house, for the ones Carolyn had seen all seemed equally fine and equally orderly.

"I keep them here," Elizabeth explained. "You may have this magazine, Carolyn."

She put a fashion magazine before Carolyn, already opened to a pair of pages covered with brightly-colored figures of women and children, all dressed in the latest fashions. Carolyn, who was accustomed to getting her paper dolls from the mail order catalogues, could immediately see the difference between them and the beautiful ones before her. She picked up the scissors eagerly and began cutting.

"Oh, Carolyn!" Elizabeth exclaimed. "Let me show you—"

She began to demonstrate the better way to do things— how to paste the page firmly down on white paper and press it until it was dry, then to cut the dolls from it carefully. Once this was done, she made a little prop for each and pasted it to the back of the figure, so it would stand alone. It was a good way to do things, Carolyn decided, better than the way she had done them before.

"I'm going to make a family," Elizabeth announced, "a mama, a papa and their children." Her face was lovely and intent as she worked. "Oh, Carolyn, you are lucky! You have brothers and sisters and a niece. There is just me in our family—I don't even have a cousin."

"Yes," Carolyn agreed. Then, not wanting Elizabeth to feel unhappy, she went on, "It's nice, but the twins do tease me a lot. And Katie is older, so she doesn't like to do the same things I do. And of course, Melinda is away from home."

"But you have them," Elizabeth said, tilting her head to one side as she regarded the doll she had just cut out. "Do you know what I am going to do when I am grown?" Not waiting for Carolyn to answer, she went on. "I'm going to marry and have children. Three girls— maybe four. Then they will have three sisters. That is what I am going to do, Carolyn Pierce. What are you going to do?"

Yesterday, Carolyn might have been tempted to say she was going to have a lilac-colored dress and a hat with a plume and a hack to make calls in—*and white kid gloves.* Now, things looked a little different to her. Elizabeth, who had either these things or the promise of them, thought them not even worthy of mentioning. Instead, she wanted what Carolyn had—brothers and sisters.

"Well," Carolyn said, "I guess I'll want to do the same things you want. Except," she added loyally, "I think I'd want some boys, too."

And she would. The twins had spent much of their life teasing her, but, in spite of this, she knew they loved her. Families needed boys and girls both.

"When we have cut out all the dolls we want," Elizabeth said, "we are going to walk downtown to the drugstore for an ice cream soda. Mama left me a whole quarter to pay for them!"

The girls picked their way along the street, stepping carefully to keep on the boards or, in some cases, the sheet iron which formed the sidewalks. When they came to the stores, it was fine, for there the front porches served as walks. Between them, however, the going was not so good.

"Papa says it's a scandal, the way this town needs sidewalks," Elizabeth said, balancing herself on a piece of board. "He's started a campaign to get them, too. And a paved street, as well. Look—" She motioned toward the muddy street. "It's lucky the drugstore is on this side," she went on, "else we'd never be able to get across to the other side."

"Yes," Carolyn agreed. And lucky they were. She couldn't have borne it had she been prevented from getting that ice cream soda!

The two girls went inside the drugstore and sat down at a small, round table. The room was cool and smelled pleasantly of drugs and of the fountain, where the ice cream and the flavorings were kept. A most entrancing odor, just as the big mirror, back of the fountain, was a most elegant sight! A man made his way toward them.

"Good afternoon, Mr. Wright," Elizabeth said. Didn't she ever forget to be correct and polite, Carolyn wondered.

"Good afternoon. And what will it be for you young ladies today?"

"A chocolate ice cream soda," they replied, almost together.

Soon he was back with their order, carrying two tall glasses with dark chocolate-y fizz on top of them. "Here you are," he said, setting the sodas before the girls.

Carolyn took the long-handled spoon he gave her and dipped carefully into the glass. She put the spoon into her mouth, savored the taste. It was wonderful—cool, smooth, rich. She felt content and even proud. Here she was, Carolyn Pierce, who had come to town a little scared, a little lonely, a little timid and uncertain about how she was going to get along when school started next fall, and already she had a friend! Already she knew how to sit down at a table and order an ice cream soda. It was all pretty grand, when she thought about it.

"You girls better hurry," Mr. Wright called to them. "Looks like it's going to rain before you can say scat to a dog. It rains here this year without half trying. Never saw it like this before."

The pair took the last sip of their sodas, then scraped the tall glasses with their spoons. Carolyn wanted to raise her glass and drain the liquid left there, but Elizabeth didn't, so she refrained, too. Together, they got up from the table, pushed their chairs back and hurried out, Elizabeth leaving her money on the way.

"It *is* going to rain," Elizabeth said. "Oh, bother—I had hoped you could come on back to the house with me."

"No," Carolyn told her new friend, "I think I'd better go home."

"I'll walk with you to where you turn off," Elizabeth said.

Actually, they finished the last block running. At the corner, they called hasty farewells and then scurried on the few blocks to their homes. Even so, the first drops of rain fell just as Carolyn raced inside the door of Melinda's house.

The rain lasted a good part of the night. By morning, however, the sun was out and the world looked bright and lovely once more. When Carolyn went out to the kitchen, Melinda was up and busy.

"I thought I'd make some cookies, Carolyn," she said. "We can take them with us when we go out home Sunday. That way, I'll prove to Papa I haven't grown to be too much of a city woman. Your breakfast is set out for you. You'll have to eat alone this morning; Dennis has already gone and Kathleen is a sleepyhead."

"You should have called me, Melinda," Carolyn protested. "I would have helped with breakfast."

"Oh, this is your vacation," Melinda told her easily.

Carolyn sat down and began eating. Melinda bustled around, sifting flour into a mixing bowl, stirring the ingredients of the cookies.

"I declare," she exclaimed suddenly, "I'm the big silly! I don't have a bit of vanilla, and these cookies won't be fit to eat without it."

"I'll go get you some," Carolyn offered.

"Well, that would be a help," Melinda told her sister. "Wear your old shoes—the streets are muddy. You'll get it at Mr. Hughes' grocery store, you know."

"Of course," Carolyn replied, a little stiffly. As if she hadn't been shopping here in Amarillo with Mama often enough to know where to buy vanilla!

"As soon as you are finished with your breakfast," Melinda said, not seeming to notice, "you can comb your hair and go. You can wear that print dress you have on— it's plenty good for running an errand."

Carolyn walked downtown, retracing the path she and Elizabeth had taken yesterday. It was a lovely day—not too hot, nor yet too cool, with the sun shining brightly and the sky a polished blue. On such days, she really loved this country. It had a new-washed look, like a house all cleaned and waiting for company. That was what it was like, really, this country—waiting for people to come, happy at having them. She liked to imagine it was extra happy this morning because of all the immigrants who were coming in now. If she tried hard, she could remember what it had been like when the Pierce family came, years ago, when she was small. Amarillo hadn't been nearly this large then, and out in the country there had been very few houses—and those so far between. It had been a good hour's ride from the Pierces to the Fosters, their nearest neighbors. Now, houses were popping up all around. Carolyn had only to look out the doors, either front or back, of the Pierce house, or out of the windows, to see other houses, some as close as two miles. The Cartwrights were that near. Carolyn wondered again what was wrong to make Bryan Cartwright so standoffish around Katie. Remembering her sister, she sighed. Visiting here in Amarillo was mighty fine, but it would be nicer if Katie could be happy, the way she used to be. Good times lost a little of their flavor, she decided, when someone in your family had a problem.

She brought herself out of her thoughts to realize she was in front of the drugstore once more, the place where she and Elizabeth had enjoyed their sodas yesterday. She paused a moment, reliving that fine experience. Then she looked around her. Across the street she saw the sign, HUGHES' GROCERY STORE. The street which she must cross had been muddy yesterday; after last night's hard rain, it was impassable. Oh dear, she had been too wrapped up in her thoughts! She should have crossed over as soon as she left Melinda's, in order to be on the right side. Now, she would have to walk back ever so far before she could find a place to cross. She certainly hadn't used her wits at all. Well, there was no choice. She turned around and began retracing her steps. On her face was written her disappointment and her displeasure with herself.

"Having troubles?" she heard someone ask.

She looked up quickly and there, sitting on a horse, was Jim Foster.

"Oh, Jim!" she exclaimed. "I can't get across the street to the grocery store and Melinda is waiting for the vanilla—" She let the nature of her woe slip out all in one quick, breathless rush.

"You certainly can't, unless you swim mud," he agreed. "Here—I'll take you."

He rode closer to the porch of the drugstore, where she stood, and extended his foot, still in the stirrup. "Come on," he said, "step up."

She had done this very same thing hundreds of times when one of the twins wanted her to mount a horse behind him. So now she put her foot on Jim's instep, just as her brothers had taught her to do. With a motion fast and deft, Jim Foster reached out and pulled her up until she sat on the horse with him, behind the saddle. This done, he turned his mount and rode the few steps across the street until they were directly in front of the grocery store.

"All right," he told her. "Here you are." So saying, he put out his foot again. As before, Carolyn stepped on it and, with his hand steadying her, sprang down to the porch in front of the store.

"Oh, thank you!" she cried warmly.

It had all been so fast, so easy with his managing things, that there wasn't a chance to say anything between the time he lifted her up and the moment he set her down. My, he was strong! It didn't seem any effort for him to pull her up and then let her down again, and she wasn't little, either. He was good-looking, too. Every bit as good-looking as Bryan.

"Oh, thank you!" she said again.

"That wasn't anything," he assured her. "I couldn't let you drown in mud, right there before my eyes."

He smiled, the lines of his face looking suddenly merry and boyish as he did so. "You'd better scoot in now and get that vanilla, or whatever it is Melinda wanted."

She went into the store quickly, made her purchase and was out again in a flash. This time, she would not have such a problem. If she went far enough, there would surely be a place where she could cross over, and so get home without muddy shoes. She would keep her eyes open.

"Get your stuff?" Jim Foster asked her.

There he was, waiting just where she had left him.

"Oh, yes," she told him.

"Well, hop up," he said. "We'll get you on the right side of the street and headed for home."

She was behind him on his horse once more, and then he was letting her down in front of the drugstore.

"You'll make it now," he assured her.

"Oh, Jim," she said, "I just can't thank you—enough—" She was suddenly shy with him. She didn't understand it—a neighbor boy she had known all her life.

"Glad to do it," he said.

41

She turned to walk off, down the street toward Melinda's.

"Carolyn," he called after her.

She stopped, turned around to face him.

"I can remember when you would have told me you were 'scruciatingly' thankful to me, or something else as high-flown," he said, grinning down at her. "By the way, what's happened to all those big words you used to throw around?"

"I don't know," she confessed. "Maybe when I got big enough to use them, I didn't want to. Wasn't I a nuisance?"

"You were right cute." He grinned at her. "All eyes and big words. Well, you'd better be getting along, or Melinda will be cross."

She had started off again when he called after her once more.

"Carolyn!" His voice had a commanding note in it.

She stopped, turned toward him.

"Don't be ashamed about using those big words," he told her. "Who do you suppose set me to studying in the first place?"

"Annie?" Carolyn asked. Annie had taught her older brothers to read, just as soon as she herself learned how from Melinda. "Annie?" she guessed again.

"No, not Annie. It was you."

"Me?" Carolyn exclaimed, unbelief in her voice.

"Yes, you. Once, when you used a big word, I asked you where you got it. And you opened your eyes wide and said you found it in the dick-sum-ary, which was a fine book and I ought to read it some time. So I did, and you were right."

Carolyn stood there, unable to answer.

"Now scoot," he told her—and rode off.

Carolyn raced home to where Melinda was waiting.

"Well," her sister said. "It took you long enough."

"I had a hard time getting across the street," Carolyn explained. "I would have had to walk almost back home if Jim Foster hadn't taken me over on his horse."

"That was nice of him," Melinda said. "But then, everyone says he's a fine boy. You can beat the eggs for me, Carolyn—that way I can get through sooner."

Carolyn washed her hands and picked up the egg beater. Round and round she whisked it, until the eggs began to show frothy white, then stiff. Like snow drifted up on the prairie. Like clouds floating in the sky.

You were right cute—all eyes and big words—who do you suppose set me to studying?

"My goodness, Carolyn," Melinda exclaimed, "you've beaten those eggs twice as long as you needed to! Here, give them to me—I want to get the cookies into the oven." As she turned them into the dough, there was a low, rumbling sound outside.

"I hope that isn't thunder. If it rains again, I don't see how we can take you home Sunday. And we have to get you and Kathleen out there some way, because Dennis and I go on Tuesday."

"Maybe it won't rain," Carolyn said hopefully.

But it did. It rained all that day and the next.

"What on earth are we going to do?" Melinda worried.

"There's just one thing we can do," Dennis told her.

"The automobile, of course, is out, with the roads as muddy as they are. But there's the train."

"The train—" Melinda echoed.

"Yes, the train. There's a freight which stops at Coleman's Switch, and it takes passengers in the caboose, now that so many immigrant families are coming in on freight trains, in order to be with their goods. Carolyn and Kathleen can go on it, and some of your folks can meet them. It's not more than three miles from your place."

"But how will they know to come?" Melinda asked.

"Jim Foster is going home this week end. He'll drop by and tell your mother, if we want him to."

All eyes and big words—

"Well," Melinda said, "I guess that's the way we'll have to work things. You see Jim, Dennis, and ask him to take the message."

THREE

"WE ARE GOING to have an adventure, Carolyn," Kathleen said solemnly. She held tightly to her young aunt's hand and looked closely at the freight train standing on the track.

"Yes," Carolyn agreed.

"We are going on a very far journey," Kathleen told Dennis and Melinda, who had brought them to the station.

"Oh, sure." Dennis grinned at her.

Actually, Carolyn herself was almost as excited as the child. She looked at the caboose, the little, houselike car at the end of the train, knowing that, in a few minutes, she and Kathleen would be sitting in it, moving off with it when the train started down the track toward Coleman's Switch, where someone would be waiting to meet them.

The last time Carolyn had ridden on a real train was when Mama had taken her three daughters back to see Grandmother in East Texas. There had been a tremendous excitement about the whole thing—the wailing of the engine as it rushed along, the smell of the lunches that people were eating from cardboard boxes, the green plush seats. Mama had decided they were to eat one meal in the dining car. Carolyn still remembered that. Eating on the train was the most elegant experience in the world! Carolyn told herself that, when she grew up, she was going to marry a man with lots and lots of money and they'd spend their time traveling on trains.

"I packed you a lunch," Melinda said, handing the box to Carolyn. "Sometimes these trains are delayed. There are cookies and some bananas and a couple of sandwiches."

This train wouldn't be like the one in which they had ridden to East Texas. Really, it shouldn't take more than an hour to get to Coleman's Switch, but, since this was a freight, it would have to sidetrack for other trains and stand on a siding until the fast ones had passed. That might take a long time. You wouldn't ride on a freight unless you had to. The immigrant families did, because then they could stay with their goods which were shipped out in the same train. Time was when Carolyn had thought immigrants were people who came across the ocean in big ships from other countries. Now she knew that, out here in the Panhandle, the word had come to mean families who had bought land through the railroads, which owned great stretches of it. Real-estate agents made the deals. A lot of families were arriving now—scarcely a week went by without at least one coming.

"This is a very far journey," Kathleen repeated. "Is your neck clean, Carolyn?"

"Yes, perfectly," Carolyn told her.

Across the child's head, Melinda and Carolyn exchanged knowing glances. "Just like you," Melinda's eyes signaled, and Carolyn's answered, "Yes, I can see it myself."

Something about this exchange made Carolyn feel very adult and pleased with herself. It was one of the things she would remember about this trip. That—and Jim Foster.

All eyes and big words—who do you suppose started me to studying?

"All aboard!" the conductor shouted.

"You'll get along fine," Melinda said. She sounded a little nervous and perhaps even unhappy, not at all like herself. "You'll manage fine—"

"Of course," Carolyn assured her. Funny thing, with Melinda standing there looking half ready to cry, almost ready to call the whole thing off, Carolyn felt years older than her sister. "Of course," she repeated firmly. "I'll look after Kathleen."

"She will be very careful with me, Mama," Kathleen said. "Here, Mama, Papa, tell me good-by so we can go."

Dennis snatched her up and kissed her. Kathleen leaned forward in his arms and Melinda kissed her, too. Then Dennis started across to the train, still carrying the child.

"I want to walk, Papa," she told him.

He put her down, and he and Melinda trailed after Carolyn and Kathleen, right up to the train.

"We will go on by ourselves," Kathleen announced.

So that is what they did, with the conductor helping them, after Dennis had set their bags on the steps.

Inside the caboose, Carolyn looked around her. It was a plain but sturdy car. There was one continuous seat running along the wall, not too soft-looking and certainly not too comfortable. There was a rusty stove at one end. Carolyn chose a place by a window and helped Kathleen up beside her. Together, they turned to wave at Dennis and Melinda, who were still standing on the platform. The engine gave a whistle. There was a rumbling, crashing sound far down the track as the engine started, pulling the car next to it which, in turn, began to move the others. With a jerk, the train started—slowly at first, then gathering speed. They were off!

When Dennis and Melinda were out of sight, Carolyn turned away from the window, and as she did so, she noticed the other people in the caboose.

There were four of them, a man and a woman and two children. The girl appeared to be a little younger than Carolyn, but perhaps that was because she was thin and rather pale, and seemed timid and uncertain. The boy was still younger—and still thinner. The mother was the thinnest of all—she actually looked ill. She rested her head against the wall of the caboose and apparently had little interest in what was going on. The man had a book in his hand. Now and then he looked up from it briefly, then started reading again. Carolyn caught the girl's eyes on her. She smiled in a friendly way. The girl's face flushed with pleasure and she, too, smiled. Perhaps they might even have started talking had not the conductor come along at that moment.

"Tickets," he said.

Carolyn got a slip of cardboard out of her purse and handed it to the man.

48

"Kathleen is not quite five," she explained. "She rides free."

"Oh, sure," the conductor replied.

"There you are, young ladies," he said, handing her back a receipt. Even as he spoke, the train slowed down, began to stop. The man across the aisle looked up from his book.

"Why are we stopping again?" he asked.

"Have to wait for Number Ten," the conductor told him.

"Wait—wait!" the man exclaimed. "That's all I've done since I got on this train."

"Well," the conductor said, not unkindly, but perhaps a little impatiently, "that's the way it goes. You ain't on a real passenger train, you know. You're on a freight, and you got your things right on this train, ready to unload at Coleman's Switch, once we pull in. Won't be long now, either."

"This Coleman's Switch—are there stores and such there?"

"No, it's just what it says—a switch where trains side-track to wait for other trains."

"Oh!" The man went back to his book.

The train remained perfectly still. Now and then there was a creaking sound, as if some parts of the engine were groaning at the weight that had been put upon them. Inside, the sound seemed as loud and big as the caboose. Kathleen moved restlessly.

"Why aren't we going, Carolyn?" she asked.

"We have to wait for another train," Carolyn explained.

"I'm hungry," Kathleen told her. "Just awfully hungry."

She couldn't be really hungry; it was too short a time since breakfast. Still, Carolyn didn't want her niece to become upset, almost before the journey had started, so she reached for the box of lunch Melinda had prepared. "You want a cooky?" she asked.

She handed one to Kathleen and took one herself.

Carolyn was never to know what made her look up, but she did, and caught the boy's eyes on her. Not on her so much as on the cooky she was eating. He was looking at it as if he could not bear to watch her and yet, at the same time, could not tear his glance away. Carolyn realized suddenly that the boy was hungry in a way she herself had never been. For the first time in her life, she was looking at a really hungry person! Kindness moved her and she spoke quickly, impulsively.

"Would you like one?" she asked the boy, at the same time extending the box toward him.

For a moment she thought he was going to throw himself in her direction. Then he looked quickly at his mother. She nodded. The boy stretched his hand out eagerly, took a cooky.

"My goodness," Kathleen said, in that wise, grown-up way of hers, "you take my sandwich. I don't want it. I don't want it at all."

Again the boy hesitated, looked at his mother. She, too, seemed to hesitate this time, but finally she nodded. The boy took the sandwich as well. Then, at a look from his mother, he said, "Thank you."

Carolyn realized that the girl was watching intently, yet trying not to act as if she were.

"Here," she said to the girl, "you take this other sandwich. My sister fixed them for us and we don't want them at all. Take it—and a cooky, too."

The girl looked at her mother; again that hesitation and again the look which gave permission. The girl, too, took the food. "Thank you," she said, and began to eat.

Carolyn extended the box in turn to the mother, who took a cooky, and to the father, who refused one. At that moment, the train gave a lurch and they were off again. The boy and girl across the caboose did not even look up —they were eating their food as if it was the first they had had in a long, long time. Carolyn found herself reluctant to watch them. She looked out the window.

The rains had made the country very green and lovely. Flowers bloomed along the right of way, especially the small yellow ones which some people said gave Amarillo its name. *Amarillo*—the Spanish word meaning "yellow." Cattle grazed in the distance and fields were green with crops that had been planted. It was all very beautiful. Carolyn wondered what this immigrant family thought of it. She turned toward them once more, just in time to see the mother slip her cooky to the boy.

"Here," Carolyn said, extending the box once more, "we might as well eat the rest of them. And the bananas."

The last bit of food was gone—sandwiches, bananas and cookies—including the boxful of the latter that Melinda had sent along for her father to prove that she had not turned into a "city girl" entirely. The family had turned to watch the country from the windows of the caboose. Someway, they looked much happier, all except the father, who didn't look much of anything.

"We should be getting home to Grandma very soon

now," Kathleen said. The girl across the caboose smiled at hearing this, and Carolyn, catching her eye, smiled back. Again, something moved Carolyn, just as it had done when she offered the cookies.

"Won't you come over here and sit with me?" she asked.

Once more the girl looked at her mother, who nodded. The girl moved over and sat down by Carolyn.

"Hello," Carolyn said.

"Hello," the girl answered shyly.

She was clean enough, Carolyn noticed, but her dress was wrinkled. It looked as if she had worn it for a long time. Her hair, very dark and smooth, was plaited in two long braids which hung down her back.

"My name is Carolyn Pierce," Carolyn told her.

"And mine is Kathleen Kennedy," Kathleen put in, not waiting for Carolyn to continue the introductions. "I was named for my grandmother and my Aunt Katie and I'm going to see them now."

The girl smiled. "My name is Rowena Warren," she said.

"That's a pretty name," Carolyn told her.

"Papa got it out of a book," the girl said proudly. "He reads lots of books."

The girl didn't look timid and frightened now. She looked proud—of herself, her name, her father. Most especially of her father. Her whole appearance had changed.

"I like to read, too," Carolyn said. "We all do—all our family."

"My brother's name came out of a book, also," Rowena went on. "His name is Ivanhoe, but he doesn't like it, so we call him Van."

"That's nice, too," Carolyn said, although she could see why a boy wouldn't want to be called Ivanhoe.

"What is this—this place called Coleman's Switch—what is it like?"

The girl seemed both anxious and fearful about knowing. She lowered her voice as she spoke, looking in her father's direction. "We—we thought it was a town, but the conductor says it isn't."

"It's like he said," Carolyn told her. "Just a place where trains meet. But they will let us off there. My folks will meet us." Then, as the thought occurred to her. "Will someone be there to meet you?"

"I think so—yes, I think the real-estate man will be there. At least, he told Papa's friend—the one who arranged for us to buy this place—that he would meet us."

"How nice," Carolyn said.

"We have bought a farm," Rowena said. Again, pride seemed to reach out and take her in its grasp. "A great, big, huge farm. We are going to live there, and Mama will get well, and we will be rich."

The train gave a whistle, began to slow down. The conductor stuck his head in at the door. "Coleman's Switch next," he told them.

"Rowena—" the mother called, a sound of excitement in her voice. For a moment she looked almost well again —and pretty, and not much older than Rowena.

The man closed his book. The boy, Van, unable to stand the suspense any longer, ran to the window and glued his nose against it. The whole family gave out a feeling of expectancy, of excitement.

Rowena started toward her mother, but paused long

enough to add something more. "A really *big* farm," she said proudly. Then, apparently having no more time for Carolyn, she started to help her family collect their bags and parcels.

Kathleen was the first one down the steps of the train, of course, but Carolyn was awfully close behind her. She looked around. Sure enough, there were Mama and Katie, standing on the platform. They rushed forward to greet the two passengers. The way they did it, you'd think nobody had seen anybody for at least a dozen years.

"Kathleen!" Mama cried. "Carolyn!"

Katie was right there with the kissing and hugging, too. It was good to be back. Oh, it *was* good to be here!

"Well," Mama finally said, "we'd better take those bags in the carriage and start home."

"I'll help you," the conductor offered, coming along at that moment.

"Oh, thank you," Mama told him as he picked up the two bags and started walking with them toward the hitch-rack where the team was tied.

Carolyn looked over her shoulder to see, now that her own excitement had died down, what was happening to the Warrens. They were standing on the platform, perfectly still, looking lost and uncertain once more. Carolyn's heart went out to them. They had thought the real-estate man would be there to meet them—and he wasn't.

"Someone was supposed to meet them," Carolyn said.

"Who?" the conductor asked. Then, following her gaze, "Oh, them immigrant people. Someone will come. We're going to switch their car of gear off here, and someone

will be along later, to help them unload and so **on.**
They've bought them a place from some smart real-estate
man."

"Oh dear!" Mama exclaimed. "I hope it's a good one."

"I think it's good enough, as such places go," the man
assured her. "I understand it has a well and a windmill
and a dugout on it. And," he added, "a creek of some
sort."

"That's wonderful!" Mama said, smiling again. "It's
a lot more than we had on our place when we first came."

"Well," the man went on, "I'll bet you knew a lot more
about managing than they do. City people—and him with
his nose in a book all the time. I think they've stuck all
their life savings into this place, because the mother isn't
well and needed to come west for her health."

"I hope she'll get better soon," Mama said.

"Did they ever have themselves a bad time coming
down!" the man continued, evidently anxious to talk to
someone about it. "That Zulu they were in was a bad
one—"

"Zulu?" Mama repeated uncertainly.

"That's what we call the cars we bring the immigrant
families out in," he explained. "Don't ask me why, we
just do. The railroad has a way of putting old, beat-up
ones off on these families, because they don't always pay
too good. The car the Warrens came in was worse than
most, so I let them ride in the caboose from Amarillo."

He paused to look back at it, switched off and standing
alone on the track now.

"It sagged in the middle. Took twelve hours to get it
across eleven miles in the Oklahoma Panhandle. By the
time they got to Amarillo this morning, they were plumb

wore out. I feel right sorry for them, I do. Only, they are so proud and standoffish like, they won't let you pity them.''

"The poor things!" Mama cried. "I'll find out where their place is and go see them, soon as they get settled. I still remember how good it was to find that I had neighbors when I first came out here." '

"It's the old Sudley claim they bought, I understand," the man said. He was putting the two bags into the surrey now.

"Oh, that," Mama said, her face clouding a little. "It's not too far from us. Oh, thank you."

"That's all right," the conductor said, and walked back to the train, which was ready to leave.

The old Sudley place. Carolyn knew about it, too. It did have those things the man had itemized—a well and a dugout and a windmill, and even a little creek. But the dugout had no roof to speak of, and the whole place was in disrepair. A family had tried to prove up the claim several years ago, had found they couldn't stick it out and had simply walked away and left it. Carolyn remembered Rowena's eyes; the proud lift of her head when she said, "A really *big* farm—we'll be rich—"

"And now," Mama exclaimed, as she got into the surrey, with Kathleen beside her and Katie in the back seat with Carolyn, "now—tell me all about your visit."

There was so much to tell. For one thing, there was Elizabeth.

"She and her mother came calling, Mama. And she had on white kid gloves and carried her own calling card!"

"To be sure," Mama said. "That's the way your grandmother and I used to do, when we made calls. I had my own cards, and I wore white kid gloves."

It seemed hard to imagine Mama back in East Texas, a little girl making calls with her own mother. All that seemed real about Mama now was her life out here in the Panhandle, managing a home and a family. Yet one day she must have been as Elizabeth was now; or even, perhaps, Carolyn herself. It was a sobering thought. Carolyn had the feeling, for no real reason, that maybe she ought to offer to help Mama more—do dishes and make beds and such things.

She told about the paper-doll cutting.

"I think that's a lovely idea," Mama said. "Making stands for them."

She told, also, about going to buy vanilla and getting stranded on the wrong side of the street. And how Jim Foster came along and took her across behind him on his horse.

"Now wasn't that nice of him!" Mama cried. "He's a real fine boy. Smart and ambitious and all that. Studies hard—"

And who was it set me to studying? He had swung her up on the horse behind him just as easily! Like a knight, rescuing a lady in distress. Like the fairy prince on the cover of that book Katie kept in her room all the time— a big, grown girl, keeping her old, worn-out book of fairy tales out in plain sight. That was a funny thing to do. Carolyn turned to look at Katie.

Her sister was still pale, maybe even a little more so than when Carolyn went away.

"Do you feel all right, Katie?" the younger girl asked.

"Why of course," Katie answered, speaking a little sharply, for her.

57

"Carolyn," Mama broke in quickly, "I tell you what we'll do. We'll invite Elizabeth out for the Fourth. There's going to be a speaking at the schoolhouse, and Dennis and Melinda will be coming anyway, to get Kathleen. I'll write Elizabeth's mother and ask her to let her daughter come with them."

"Oh, Mama!" Carolyn cried breathlessly. "Oh, Mama!"

"And I'll go see those—what did you say their names were?"

"Warren," Carolyn told her.

"I'll go see them and take a pie, or something."

"Oh, that is wonderful, Mama!"

The hurt of remembering Rowena's face as she told how rich they were going to be was relieved a little now, with Mama's kindness in prospect.

"You have not said any words to me for a long time," Kathleen announced reprovingly.

"And so I haven't, my darling," Mama agreed. "Now you must talk to me. How did you like traveling on a caboose?"

"It was very good," she said. "But I am hungry. The little boy ate all my cookies. He was the hungriest boy I have ever seen. He ate everything—even the cookies Mama sent Grandpa."

"There are oodles and oodles of cookies at Grandma's," Mama reassured her. "I baked them especially for you!"

"Then drive fast, please, for I am hungry," Kathleen begged her.

"That I will," Mama said.

She gave the horses a smart slap with the lines. The wheels began to spin faster. Not long now, and they'd be home. Carolyn thought she couldn't wait. Yet, even as the picture of her own well-kept home came to her, she was wondering how the Warrens would feel when the real-estate man let them out at the Sudley place, with the sagging roof and the fences tumbled down and all the rest of the unkempt look of it.

FOUR

"CAN'T YOU DRIVE FASTER, Grandpa?" Kathleen asked. "We will be late."

Papa smiled. He knew everyone was anxious to get to the schoolhouse, where the Fourth of July speaking was going to be held, as well as the dinner on the grounds and all sorts of excitement.

"We'll be there in a minute, honey," he told her.

Sure enough, it was only a short time until the surrey drew up in front of the fence which surrounded the schoolyard.

Even before Papa stopped to let them out, Carolyn could see that Dennis and Melinda had not yet arrived. There was no automobile waiting in front of the schoolhouse.

Kathleen said, "My mama and papa are not here yet."

"They will be, honey," Mama assured her. "They'll be here, soon."

Of course they would! Carolyn wanted to see them, naturally, but it wasn't for their own sakes alone, this time. When they came, Elizabeth would be with them. Mama had written Mrs. Lindley to ask whether her daughter could come out with Dennis and Melinda for a visit, as she had promised, and Elizabeth's mother had replied that she might. Just thinking about it all made Carolyn shiver with excitement and delight.

Even though Dennis and Melinda and Elizabeth had not yet arrived at the schoolhouse, a great many other people had. Tables were being spread and baskets unpacked. Over in one corner of the yard, a stand had been set up where ice cream and soda pop could be bought. A platform had been erected, with a speaker's stand on it, and an American Flag. Men and women stood around in knots, talking, and children raced about the yard like fish in a pond, not because they had any place to go but because they simply had to keep in motion. It was all very exciting and different from the way things looked when school was going on.

Papa tied the team securely to the hitchrack, where other teams and riding horses were already standing. He helped Mama out, lifted Kathleen and set her on the ground. Carolyn clambered out by herself, then followed Mama to where the tables stood, carrying a small basket in her hands. Papa brought the big basket of food. Katie walked along, holding very carefully a big bouquet she had fixed to put in the center of the picnic table.

"Oh, what pretty flowers!" the women exclaimed when she came near. "How do you do, Mrs. Pierce?"

"How do you do?" Mama replied.

"They shouldn't have done it," Mrs. Cartwright was saying. She was a great talker, Mrs. Cartwright was. She stopped just long enough to greet the Pierces, then went on, "I say they shouldn't have done it."

Meg Cartwright, who had been standing close to her mother, detached herself from the group and came to Carolyn. "Hello," she said brightly. Meg was a year younger, but she was awfully jolly and good company. "Oh, my," she exclaimed, "isn't it all wonderful? I just love the Fourth of July!"

"I do, too," Carolyn told her.

The Fourth of July was wonderful because of what it meant to the whole country, Carolyn was thinking. But it was good, too, because it was celebration time. Today it meant a picnic dinner and afterwards the speaking, and in the evening some fireworks—not a lot of magnificent ones, like they had in town, but at least some. Carolyn could remember the first Fourth the Pierces had spent here in the Panhandle. They had gone on a plum-picking picnic, and Melinda and Katie got lost. What a lot of excitement that had caused! Mama wanting to cry but being brave; Papa and all the men and boys going out to look for the lost ones. Melinda had had sense enough to start singing, or they never would have found them until morning, dark as it was. Melinda always did think of something. And Katie followed her, no matter what she wanted to do.

Katie looked lovely today. She was standing by Mama, wearing a flowered dress and a hat with morning-glories on it. Her eyes kept roving around the crowd, looking for someone. Carolyn knew, without being told, who it was.

"Oh, hello, Katie," Mrs. Cartwright said. "You certainly do look pretty."

Bryan might not pay much attention to Katie, but his mother liked her. Katie flushed with pleasure at her compliment.

"Anyway," Mrs. Cartwright went on, "as I was saying, I think it was awful for them to do it—"

She always spoke her mind firmly, without wavering. "It's a downright shame," she declared.

"What?" Mama asked. She was a great one for getting at the bottom of things.

"The way those Adams boys treated the new family—the Warrens."

Carolyn pricked up her ears. That was the family she had met in the caboose on the way home from Amarillo. It was funny about them—Mama had gone over there in a day or two, taking a big pie with her. She had knocked and knocked, but nobody came to the door.

"Maybe they had all gone somewhere," Papa suggested when Mama came back with her pie still in her basket.

"Maybe," Mama answered, "but I had the strangest feeling that they were there, inside the house, and wouldn't come to the door. And what a terrible condition that house is in, to be sure!"

"Well," Papa said, "all is not lost. We can eat the pie."

They did, but some way, it didn't have as much flavor as usual for Carolyn. Now, here was Mrs. Cartwright with a story to tell about the Warrens. Maybe it would explain why they didn't come to the door when Mama called.

"It wouldn't have been so bad," Mrs. Cartwright went

on now, unwilling to be hurried, "if they hadn't been city people, from Chicago I hear, and not knowing one little thing about the country—"

"My goodness!" Mama exclaimed. "Tell us what happened!"

"Those Adams boys," Mrs. Cartwright explained. "You know what they are like—"

Naturally, everyone knew the Adams boys—Hank and Cy. They were always full of pranks and rough jokes. They had been real problems when they first started to school, although, after a while, Mr. Palmer had tamed them down a little. Big, lumbering, good-natured boys, there was no real harm in them, but they did make life miserable for people who didn't know how to take them.

"Well, they went over to the Warren place and told Mr. Warren, almost the first day he moved in, that there was a dead man down at the corner of his fence. It was dark and pouring rain, but poor Mr. Warren started out to look for him, and he looked and looked—all over the place—"

A dead man! How was Mr. Warren to know, new as he was to the country, that this was the name given to a brace for a fence post. How ridiculous he must have felt when he spent all that time looking and found nothing at all!

"Poor things!" Mama cried. "I took them a pie, but there was nobody at home. At least, they didn't come to the door."

"Well, if you couldn't get any better reception than I did, you can be glad nobody came. I took a loaf of bread and a cake. The children were out in the yard. I asked if their mother was at home and they said they'd call their father. He came to the door, looking as if he thought I was trying to poison the family. He didn't even ask me in. Finally, I just pushed the stuff into his hands and turned and left. I wasn't going to force my way inside."

"Poor things!" Mama exclaimed again. "It isn't easy to come to a new country."

"Well, nobody asked them to come," Mrs. Cartwright said practically, "so they needn't take it out on us. But all the same, I think those horrid Adams boys did wrong."

"Let's see what's going on," Meg suggested to Carolyn, jumping up and down in sheer excitement. Meg was quick and brisk in all her movements, like her mother. She didn't want to stand here in one spot and listen to the women talking.

Carolyn followed Meg away. Scarcely had they detached themselves from the group when someone called out, "There they come!"

And sure enough, there was Dennis' automobile, coming down the road, with another one following close behind.

"The speaker," someone said. "I bet that's him."

It probably would be Mr. Gaines, the speaker, all right. He was running for the senate, or something, wanting to go down to Austin and help make the laws. He thought today would be a good chance for him to meet voters. Carolyn wasn't interested in him at all. She kept her eyes on Dennis' automobile, for in it Elizabeth would be riding. She grasped Meg's hand and together they raced toward the automobiles, which drove up and stopped.

Kathleen stood with Mama, waiting. Seeing her, Melinda was out in a flash and rushing toward her little daughter. Carolyn looked past them, and there, sure enough, was Elizabeth.

She looked just the way Carolyn remembered her—very

65

pretty and extremely neat. Her dress was like one of those pictures the girls had cut out of the style magazine, and she wore a little hat and, yes, gloves—but not kid ones. They were white cotton, because this was a picnic. Carolyn felt a little shy, all of a sudden. She said, without moving, "Hello, Elizabeth."

"Hello, Carolyn," Elizabeth responded, coming to her side. "Oh, it is good to see you!"

"This is my friend, Meg Cartwright," Carolyn told her.

"Hello," Meg said briskly. "We're awfully glad you came. We're going to have lots of fun while you're here."

It was good to be like Meg, Carolyn thought—always happy and even-tempered and never shy about things. She reached out, put her arms around Elizabeth and squeezed her tightly. "It *is* nice, Elizabeth," she said. "Oh, I'm so glad you could come!"

The three of them started toward the schoolyard. Then it was that Carolyn noticed the occupants of the second automobile. The speaker, Mr. Gaines, a portly man with a bald head, was beginning to shake hands with everyone. And there, just sliding from under the wheel, was Jim Foster. He went over to the men, passing close to Carolyn and not seeming to see her at all. Well, why should he, Carolyn thought. I'm just a child—a little neighbor girl he helped across the street one day—someone he's known all his life and never noticed much. For a moment she felt dissatisfied with herself and with the day. She didn't have much place here. She was too old to run around with the children, darting all over the place, and she was too young to be noticed by the grownups.

"Do you know," Elizabeth said, "I have never been **to**

66

a speaking before. I have never been out in the country—"

She realizes I'm upset about something, Carolyn
thought. She's trying to make me feel better about her
being here. That was Elizabeth—polite, correct, thoughtful. Maybe this visit wasn't going to turn out as well as
Carolyn had hoped. Maybe Elizabeth would get tired of
the country, with no excitement at all, the way there was
in town.

"Well," Carolyn told her city friend, "I hope you like
it—"

The picnic dinner was finished. Everybody had eaten
so much it was a wonder they could move at all. Mr.
Gaines walked around among the crowd, talking with
people. Talk is what he had come to do, and nothing
was going to stop him. He went over to Dennis, said a
few words. Dennis nodded, and together the two of them
mounted the platform. Dennis went to the speaker's stand
and Mr. Gaines seemed happier, now that he knew he was
going to have his chance to tell the people why they
should vote for him.

Dennis rapped for order, at ease, as always. Slowly, the
buzz of talk died down, and people began to draw closer
to the platform. Women sat on the benches scattered
around. For the most part, the men and children and
young people lounged on the grass or stood. Meg drew
Carolyn and Elizabeth after her. "I know just the place,"
she said. "We can have a seat and still see everything."

The place she had found was the schoolhouse steps,
and a very good one it was. The three girls sat down together just as Dennis began speaking.

"Friends and neighbors," he said, "it's mighty good to see you here today. We have a few announcements before we get to the speaker. Jim Foster, where are you?"

Jim Foster made his way to the platform.

"Oh, my goodness," Elizabeth whispered to Carolyn, "isn't he nice looking?"

He certainly was. He was dressed up in his very best, and he moved and acted as though he were every bit as much at ease as Dennis was.

"We are going to have a baseball game after the speaking," Jim said. "The married men will play the single ones. Dr. Kennedy will be captain of the married ones and I'm the leader of the single fellows. Of course," he added, "I reckon if you don't like your captains, you can put us out. But I warn you—it won't be easy."

Everyone laughed a lot at that; you'd have thought he had said something tremendously funny. But then, people were ready to laugh at anything today, they were so happy and at peace with their fellow men.

"No complaints?" he went on, when the laughter had died down. "All right—then I'll meet my team east of the schoolhouse. Dr. Kennedy can take his to the west side, or wherever he wants. They don't have a chance, anyway, against us bachelors."

"Now don't be too sure about that," Dennis put in. "West suits us fine."

"Remember," Jim continued, "all those who want to play, report at the proper places as soon as the speaking is over."

He walked down off the platform with everyone clapping away as if he had made a really fine speech. Mr. Gaines looked a little upset. He probably suspected that the people would listen to him just to be polite, but all the time they would hardly be able to wait for him to finish so the ball game could start.

"Jim Foster talks awfully well," Elizabeth declared. "My father said we are to keep our eyes on that young man. He's going to make something out of himself."

"Of course," Meg said, not wanting to be left out of anything. "Papa says he's the flower of the Foster flock."

Carolyn listened, pride taking over in her heart. It was Jim Foster they were talking about, a boy she had known ever since she had come to the Panhandle. It was almost like having one of the twins praised—well, not quite, but almost. She felt warm and happy and pleased to have Elizabeth see that, even though they lived out here in the country, thirty miles from town, they were still capable and smart.

And who do you think started me studying?

She wished she might tell Elizabeth what Jim had said, and Meg, too, but she didn't quite dare. It would seem like bragging on her part. Besides, when she didn't tell anyone, just hugged the memory to her heart, it was a beautiful secret, to be cherished and guarded. More fun, really.

"All right," Dennis began, once Jim was off the platform, "Now we are going to have a real privilege. The Honorable Mr. Gaines will speak to us. We all know him and respect him, so I won't take up his time talking about him. You know, too, that he wants us to elect him to the senate, so he can get away from this part of the country. He doesn't care for it, so he wants to go down to Austin."

During the laughter that followed, Mr. Gaines made his way to the speaker's stand. Austin was the capitol and that was where he wanted to be, Carolyn was thinking, but not because he didn't like the Panhandle. Austin was a lovely town; some of these days Carolyn was going to see it for herself. The capitol and the university and all the beautiful homes. Annie knew her way around among all that loveliness—and, before long, Jim would, too.

"Now, friends," Mr. Gaines began, "Dr. Kennedy is a fine man, but you can't always believe him. He grew up out here among you, so I don't have to tell you that."

More laughter.

"You know, as well as I do, that I think this is the finest country in the world. The very best—"

Carolyn ceased to follow him. The best country in the world! It was that to her, because she had little memory of any other place. Mama liked it, too, although Carolyn suspected that at first she hadn't been too much pleased with the wind and no trees and few neighbors and the vast, blank stretches of level land reaching out in every direction. All the Pierce children loved it, however, and wouldn't live anywhere else.

Her mind skipped quickly to the Warrens. What would they say to Mr. Gaines's words? To them, it must seem anything but a wonderful country. Yet, how would they get to know how nice the people were if they didn't let them inside their house?

And Elizabeth, how was she going to feel about these people out here in the country? Carolyn wished she could tell her new friend that Mama used to make calls with her own mother, wearing white gloves and carrying her own cards. Only she couldn't, for that, also, would have been bragging, and Mama said you never did that. She said that if you amounted to anything, people would find it out; and, if you didn't, you could say you did until you were black in the face and nobody would believe you.

Besides, Carolyn thought the way Mama did things was right and good out here. Her mother didn't carry calling cards any more when she went to see her neighbors, but she took pies instead, or homemade bread, or something they would enjoy. And if anyone was sick or needed her, Mama never waited to go and help. Cards and white kid gloves would have been silly, here in the country. Carolyn was proud of Mama because she could fit into the life here.

"And so," Mr. Gaines was saying, just as Carolyn began to listen once more, "I think we'll conclude this meeting by singing 'The Star Spangled Banner.' Anyone here to lead us?"

He turned to consult with Dennis, then faced the audience once more.

"Will Miss Katie Pierce be good enough to come forward?" he asked.

From where she was sitting, Carolyn could see Katie flush and then turn pale. Mama, next to her, gave her a little nudge. Katie looked at her uncertainly, and Mama nodded vigorously. Katie started toward the platform. Dennis met her and escorted her across the stage, to the center. My she looked pretty, Carolyn thought, like a fair lady in a picture. The blue morning-glories on her hat matched the blue-flowered dress she wore, and her eyes were a darker blue than either. She looked just like a doll, a life-sized doll. Her cheeks had begun to grow pink once more, the way they always did when there was a chance for her to sing. Her hair curled softly. Carolyn was so proud of her she could scarcely stand it.

71

"Your sister is a beautiful girl!" Elizabeth exclaimed.

"Oh, yes," Carolyn agreed. It was perfectly all right to say that about your own sister, especially when it was true.

Katie lifted her hand and everyone grew quiet.

"I'll start," she said, "and then you must all sing with me. Ready—"

She began to sing. Her voice rang out, clear and true and very lovely. People joined in the singing, but always, above them all, Carolyn could hear Katie's voice. When they came to the high notes almost everyone stopped singing, but Katie never faltered. The flag behind her rippled out in the wind; the sky above her was brightly blue. As far as Carolyn could see, back of the stage, the green fields of the Panhandle stretched on and on, forever on, until they met the sky and their green was one with the sky's blue.

Carolyn didn't know why she looked away from Katie at that particular moment, but she did. The thing she saw made her wonder. There stood Bryan Cartwright, not singing at all, but looking at Katie as if he were trying to fill his eyes with the sight of her. As if, maybe, he were getting ready to rush up there to her, the minute she had finished leading the song, and pick her up and carry her off with him. Carolyn didn't know which one to watch—Bryan, on the ground, or Katie, on the platform.

She remembered how Bryan was all tied up with the Pierces, and especially with Katie. Little things came back to her—Bryan bringing the news of Mrs. Lister's illness and almost breaking up Melinda and Dennis' wedding; Bryan, happening in the time Katie burned her hand and putting soda on it; Bryan, helping Katie at school when things got difficult. Always, always, that's the way things had been. Now he stood there watching Katie with his heart in his eyes—yet when he was around her, he scarcely spoke to her!

Katie had finished, was walking down off the platform. People clapped and clapped. The noise seemed to bring Bryan back to himself. He shook off that look he had worn, and, by the time Katie was on the ground, he was as cool and detached as ever.

In coming back to where Mama sat, Katie passed close to him. She seemed almost ready to stop; her hand went to her throat in a quick, helpless gesture.

"Hello," she said, speaking uncertainly.

"Hello," Bryan replied softly. "Katie, you—"

Then he did the rudest thing. He broke off, turned around and started walking away, very fast, toward the east side of the schoolhouse, where Jim Foster's baseball team was already gathering. Katie turned red, then white. Slowly, almost as if she didn't know where she was going, she walked on toward Mama.

"My mama says my brother Bryan is a big silly," Meg interrupted Carolyn's thoughts. "She tells him and she tells him—"

"The game is going to start," Carolyn broke in. "Let's go watch."

She knew what Meg meant to say, and not for worlds would she let her get those words out. Mrs. Cartwright thought Bryan was a big silly because he didn't pay any attention to Katie. Carolyn herself would give a great deal to know what had happened between them. Ever since Katie came back from school it had been like this. Something had happened, all right, but that was Katie's secret and Carolyn wasn't going to let Meg talk about it.

"All right," Meg said.

Together the three girls—Meg and Elizabeth and Caro-lyn—walked over to the place where the baseball game was about to begin.

FIVE

CAROLYN WOKE UP to the deliciously wonderful feeling that this was the day when something nice was going to happen. She stretched her arms above her head, turned in bed—and then she knew it had already happened. She was in the spare room bed and, beside her, still fast asleep, was Elizabeth Lindley.

Asleep, Elizabeth was as beautiful and as correct as when she was awake. Her hair, which she had brushed a full one hundred strokes the night before (she had counted them out loud and Carolyn knew she hadn't skipped a one) was plaited in two smooth braids—still just as smooth as they had been when she went to bed last night. Her nightgown looked as if she had not turned over all night long. Beside her, Carolyn felt frowzy and unkempt. She put one foot over the edge of the bed, thinking to slip out quietly, hoping to get her hair brushed, her face washed, before Elizabeth saw her. She had no luck. The first small motion on her part and Elizabeth was awake.

"Oh, dear," she said, sitting gracefully erect, "is it morning?"

"Yes," Carolyn told her, standing out on the floor by now.

"But—it seems so early—"

"We get up early in the country," Carolyn explained.

"Oh, that's right. Mama told me—"

She, too, was out of bed now. She went over to the washbowl, poured out water from the pitcher. She washed her face and hands thoroughly. She combed her hair, although it didn't need anything done to it at all. Then she went to her bag and began to take out fresh underwear. Every single thing she put on, Carolyn knew, would be freshly laundered. Carolyn, who was ready to jump into the clothes she had worn yesterday morning, before she dressed for the picnic, thought better of it.

"I'll go to my room to dress," she said. "My things are in there. You see, I room with Katie."

"Oh, how nice," Elizabeth said, "having a sister to room with!"

"Yes," agreed Carolyn thoughtfully, "it truly is. When you are dressed," she told her friend, "go out to the kitchen. I'll be there in a jiffy."

The two girls walked into the kitchen at almost the same minute. Katie was washing the dishes; Mama was moving about, putting things to right.

"Good morning," they all chorused together.

"What would you like for breakfast?" Mama asked.

76

"Whatever you are having for the family," Elizabeth answered politely.

"We've eaten—ages ago," Mama told her.

"Oh!" Elizabeth said a little uncertainly.

"You're in the country now." Mama smiled at her. "Here, we eat early."

"Yes, ma'am," Elizabeth responded. "I mean, it is nice to start a day off early—"

She'd be polite, Carolyn was thinking, if we knocked her down and stepped on her. She'd remember to say thank you when we let her up! I'd like to see something happen that would jar her out of that politeness. Then, immediately, she was ashamed of herself. She really liked Elizabeth. She liked her a lot. It was good to have her visiting here. And if she, Carolyn, was smart, she would try to learn some of those nice, smooth, polite ways herself.

"Here's some oatmeal for you," Mama said, putting two bowls on the table. "Sit down and start on that while I fry you an egg."

Elizabeth and Carolyn sat down, facing each other across the table. Each took a taste at the same time.

"This is delicious oatmeal," Elizabeth said.

"It's the country cream on it," Mama said. "Now what do you girls plan to do today, once you've finished breakfast?"

Elizabeth swallowed the food she had in her mouth. She raised her napkin to her lips, wiping them daintily. "Oh, whatever Carolyn wants to do," she answered.

"I thought we'd go riding, Mama," Carolyn told her mother. "I thought we'd go over to Meg's and ask her to go with us. Would it hurt if we got home a little late for dinner?"

"Not a bit," Mama replied cheerfully. "I'll pack you some cookies and an apple apiece in a bag. Then you won't starve before you get back. It's a nice day for a ride—not too hot."

"Would it be all right if Elizabeth rode your horse, Katie?"

"Of course," Katie said. "I'd love to have her ride him."

"I—I don't know much about riding—or horses—or things like that," Elizabeth said. She looked scared when she said it.

"I'll show you," Carolyn told her. "You'll learn quickly. Katie rides a sidesaddle, and that's easy. Just like sitting in a rocking chair. You can borrow her riding skirt, too."

Carolyn couldn't imagine Elizabeth riding as she herself did—astride, wearing a divided skirt.

It wasn't any time until the two girls were ready for the ride, Elizabeth in Katie's long skirt, Carolyn wearing her own divided one. They made their way toward the corral where the horses were kept. Out of the corner of her eye, Carolyn could see how pale Elizabeth was, and, all at once, the prospect of riding lost some of its flavor.

"Elizabeth," she said, "you don't have to ride if you don't want to. We can stay here and cut paper dolls, or do something else."

"I'll ride," Elizabeth declared. She might be pale, but she was determined. "I'll ride," she repeated.

"All right," Carolyn said, liking her city friend even better than she had before, which was liking her a lot.

"You climb on the corral gate and I'll lead your horse close so you can mount without any trouble."

Elizabeth caught up the long riding skirt, climbed the gate. "I'm ready," she announced.

Actually, she managed better than Carolyn would have thought possible. A moment's hesitation while she seemed to be gathering herself together, and then she was in the saddle, sitting very straight and stiff.

"Don't be afraid," Carolyn urged her. "Brownie is a very gentle horse. Katie is afraid of horses, so she must have a quiet one."

"I'm not afraid," Elizabeth declared proudly. But, although she was sitting a little easier in the saddle, she was still pale around the mouth.

When the two girls rode up to the Cartwright place, Meg ran out to meet them.

"Oh," she cried, "I'm glad you came! Hello, Carolyn. Hello, Elizabeth."

"Hello," they both said.

"My goodness, Elizabeth, you look just like Katie on that horse! She always acts as if she thinks a horse is going to bite her, or something—"

Carolyn found words of defense rising to her lips.

"Elizabeth is learning fine," she said. "She has never been on a horse before, but she is learning fast as anything."

Elizabeth's grateful look in her direction made Carolyn have a nice, warm feeling around her heart.

"Well," Meg said, "that's good. Oh, and what are you doing here?" This to Bryan, who had just walked up. He looked quickly at Elizabeth, and then he looked away, sort of disappointed and relieved, all at the same time. He didn't answer Meg, who went on briskly. "Anything wrong, Bryan? What are you doing at the house this time of the morning?"

"I wanted a drink," he told her. "You don't mind, do you?"

"I thought you took a jug of water to the field with you."

"What if I did?" he asked, reaching out to rumple her hair in a way that always made her furious. "You don't want your only brother to die of thirst, do you?"

"Oh, quit!" she cried, trying to dodge. She did not come back to the subject of his drink. But even so, Carolyn felt she understood. Bryan, too, had thought that it was Katie, on her own horse. He had come to the house to see for himself. Why was he acting so strangely, anyway? Carolyn would give a great deal to know.

"Come along with us, Meg," Carolyn urged. "We're going for a ride. Mama fixed us some cookies and stuff."

"I'll ask my mama for some, too," Meg said. "I'll ask her if I can go. Now just you wait—I'll be right back—"

She didn't seem to have any doubts about securing permission to go on the ride.

A short while later, the three girls rode off, with Mrs. Cartwright calling after them to be good and not to go too far away and to have a fine time. She was always calling directions and admonitions after her children as long as she could see them. But she was awfully nice, too, jolly and good fun and big-hearted as she could be. "My mama says my brother Bryan is a big silly—" Meg's words came back to Carolyn. Whatever made him be so distant around her sister, when all the time his family and Katie's

family and even Katie herself showed how much they
wanted him to be friends with her, the way he had been
when they were growing up together? And, remembering how Bryan had come racing to the house when he saw
Katie's horse out in front, Carolyn wondered if maybe he
didn't want to be friends, too.

Well, if he did, and yet went on acting the way he was,
maybe he was every bit the big silly his mother had called
him.

"Where'll we go?" Meg asked, breaking in on Carolyn's thoughts.

"Do you want to go anywhere special?" Carolyn asked
Elizabeth politely. After all, she was a guest.

"Oh, no," Elizabeth answered. "I don't know any place
to go." Her eyes were fixed ahead, her hands tight on
the reins.

"Loosen the reins a little, Elizabeth," Meg told her.
"My gracious—Brownie couldn't run off if he wanted to!
Just let him have his head—he'll stay with our horses."

"Yes," Elizabeth agreed meekly. She let the reins go
slack and took her eyes off the horse to turn to Carolyn.
"This is more fun—" she said. "I mean, this is more fun
than I've ever had. I am not a bit afraid."

"Of course not," Carolyn assured her. "Brownie is as
safe as anything."

"I was afraid at first," Elizabeth admitted. "I thought
I would rather die than get on a horse. But I'm not afraid
now," she finished, making a kind of song of it.

"You got over being afraid quickly," Meg said. "Katie
still looks scared to death of a horse, and she's been riding ever since she was ten years old. My brother used to

think it was sort of cute, for her to be scared of things. But I haven't heard him mention it lately."

"You're doing fine," Carolyn told Elizabeth quickly. She didn't want Meg to start on Bryan and Katie again. "I think you're real brave to ride off like this, the first time you ever got on a horse."

"Oh, thank you!" Elizabeth exclaimed. Her face flushed bright with pleasure. "You're a very lovely girl, Carolyn. I am glad I have you for a friend." She was conscious of Meg, riding along beside her. "And you, too, Meg," she added graciously.

"Well, thank you," Meg replied and, for once, was made silent with pleasure.

The silence held as the three rode along with the horses' hoofs making a nice plopping sound on the road. They were by themselves, which made them feel adult and independent, but there was, also, the sight of houses comfortably close, so that they did not feel lost or isolated. Once again, Carolyn thought back to the time when the Pierces first came to the Panhandle. There hadn't been a house for miles around then. No schoolhouse or church, either. No trees and no windmills. Nothing much but the Pierces' dugout and then, six miles or more away, the Fosters'. The ranch house, where Dennis had lived with his aunt and uncle, had seemed on the other side of the world, although, actually, it wasn't farther than twelve miles or so.

"Look!" Meg cried excitedly. She pointed as she spoke, toward a bump on the face of the prairie. "Look!" she repeated. "There's the Warrens' place—you know, that new immigrant family."

The dugout was no more than half a mile away,

crouched in a rise in the prairie, so that the back part of it was the earth itself. The front was made of wood, with dirt chinked into the cracks, just the way the Pierce dugout had been—in fact, the way the back still was, for when Papa built the new house, he had simply put it in front of the dugout. The room Katie and Carolyn shared now was part of the old dugout, as was the guest room Elizabeth and Carolyn were using during the former's visit. There was nothing wrong with the dugout—it was warm in winter, cool in summer.

"I tell you what let's do," Meg suggested. "Let's go see them. There's a girl—maybe she's our age. I wonder what her name is."

"It's Rowena," Carolyn said, before she thought.

"Well, how do you know so much about her?" Meg asked.

"I met her—the family—that day I came out on the train."

"Carolyn Pierce," Meg told her severely, "why ever did you keep so quiet about it?"

Carolyn didn't answer. Why hadn't she mentioned the meeting? Actually, she didn't know.

"It's downright rude for you not to go see her, Carolyn," Meg declared. "You ought to go and take us with you."

Carolyn shifted uncomfortably on her horse. Meg knew as well as she did that the Warrens apparently didn't want company. Both their mothers had gone, only to be ignored.

"They don't seem to like company," she said. "You know—when your mother went—and mine—"

"But that was different," Meg declared. "The Warrens

hadn't had time to get settled yet, and they are from Chicago and city people don't like company rushing in on them until they've got everything all nice and straight. Do they?" she asked, turning to Elizabeth for confirmation of her statement.

"Well—my mother always says you have to allow people time to get things in place before you rush in," Elizabeth admitted.

"What did I tell you?" Meg turned to Carolyn triumphantly. "We will see the girl—what's her name?"

"Rowena," Carolyn supplied uneasily.

"We'll see Rowena," Meg planned. "We don't have to fool around with the father at all. Look, she's playing out in the yard right this minute. She'd be hurt if she saw you ride past without stopping."

"I don't think we ought—" Carolyn hesitated. "If our mothers couldn't get in—"

"Why, Carolyn Pierce," Meg stormed, "I believe you are scared. You're as scared as your sister Katie would be."

That did it!

"All right," Carolyn said. "Let's go."

In order to get to the Warren place, the trio had to ride through a slight dip in the land, a little draw which, when rains came, was a creek of sorts. Because water sometimes stood there, a few hackberry trees had sprung up at the edge of the stream. The road crossed near the clump of trees. At this point, there was a small hollowed-out place in the side of the creek which bore evidence of use. A box was there, seeming to serve as a chair of sorts, and a few tin cans. Maybe Rowena uses this for an out-door playhouse, Carolyn thought.

As the three riders crossed the little draw, the dugout was, for a moment, hidden from them. When the road again emerged, so they could see the house, no one was visible at all.

"Well, that's funny!" Meg exclaimed. "A minute ago they were out in the yard. Now there isn't anyone in sight."

She was right. The two young Warrens, Rowena and Van, who had been out in the yard when the three girls started across the creek, weren't there now.

"Maybe they went into the—that shed, to gather eggs or something," Elizabeth supplied helpfully.

That could be. A dilapidated little building with a broken fence around it stood back of the house. There weren't any chickens in sight, just a thin-looking cow, which didn't seem a bit happy about being there. No horses, either. How did Mr. Warren expect to run his farm without horses?

The top door to the dugout was open. That wasn't strange. Mostly those doors did stay open until night came. Dugouts were like cellars; there was an outside door which folded over, and then some steps. You went down these until you came to the real door of the dugout itself. There were two windows above the ground, one on each side, just as there had been in the Pierces' dugout. Carolyn knew all about dugouts. Meg didn't, for the Cartwrights had built a house right at first.

"They saw us coming and went inside," Carolyn began.

"That's why we *have* to go on," Meg pointed out practically. "If we didn't go see them now, when we are right at their door, they would think it was funny."

The girls rode close to the house. There was still no sign of any person about, no sight or sound.

"We will get off our horses," Meg said. "And we will all go to the door."

"Oh, dear!" Elizabeth protested. "I can't, Meg. I couldn't get back on. I had to mount from the gate this morning, and then Carolyn helped me."

"We will both help you," Meg promised, "and you won't need a gate."

It was a foolish thing they were doing. Carolyn knew it, felt it. She was letting Meg take over, letting Meg lead her into something she didn't want to do. She realized this—and yet a stronger thing than that knowledge pushed her on. The three girls dismounted and walked toward the door.

"You knock," Meg directed Carolyn, "and you do the talking. After all, you've met them."

Carolyn wanted to point out that, although this might be true, it had been Meg's idea to pay this call.

"Unless you're scared—" Meg said.

Carolyn reached out, rapped on the facing to the outside door. There was no answer. She waited, then rapped again. This time she could hear footsteps inside the dugout—then guarded voices.

"Rowena," Carolyn called, "it's me. Carolyn Pierce—the one you met in the caboose that day."

The door opened, but it was not Rowena who stood there. It was Mr. Warren himself.

"Go away," he said.

"Oh, Papa!" Carolyn could hear Rowena's protest, although she could not see the girl. "Oh, Papa—she's the one who gave us the cookies and things—"

"I said—*go away!*"

"You are very rude." The voice came from close behind Carolyn. She started, looked around. Elizabeth stepped forward, until she stood at Carolyn's side. She was pale, but she spoke firmly. "You must not act like that to Carolyn," she went on. "She is only trying to be kind. *You ought to be ashamed of yourself!*"

The door closed, slam-bang in their faces. But not before Carolyn had managed a quick glance at the inside of that dugout. There wasn't much of anything in it— two pallets on the floor, a stove, a couple of chairs, a table, a bed. Mrs. Warren lay on the bed and, even in the half-light of the dugout, Carolyn could see how ill she looked. She could see, too, Rowena's face—miserable and unhappy at the way her father was acting.

"Well," Meg sputtered, "of all the hateful people—"

The girls were back on their horses once more, riding away from the Warren dugout. Elizabeth, amazingly enough, had required very little help in mounting.

"I shouldn't have done it," Carolyn said. "I knew they didn't want company. I shouldn't have gone up there and knocked."

"I'd like to know why not," Meg said. "They are newcomers, and you had met them before. It was your *duty* to call on them."

"It was wrong of me," Carolyn insisted. "Rowena looked positively crushed at the way her father acted."

"Don't you feel bad," Elizabeth told her, riding close to pat her hand gently. "You meant to be kind—"

Carolyn, remembering the taunt from Meg which had been the real reason for her knocking at the door, was silent.

"Whatever made him act like that, I wonder?" Meg asked.

"I—I don't know," Carolyn answered, the memory of Rowena's stricken face before her.

"I'll bet they are Hiding From The Law," Meg said, her eyes round with excitement, shaping every word so that it sounded as if it started with a capital letter. "I'll bet they have a treasure buried right there in the floor of the dugout, and they don't want anybody to know about it."

"Oh, Meg!" Carolyn laughed in spite of herself.

"Well, I'll bet they do. Either that, or they are Fleeing From Justice. There is a mystery there, Carolyn Pierce, and before this summer is over, I'm going to find out what it is."

No mystery, Carolyn thought. Just a sick woman and a bitter man and two unhappy children. But Meg was right—there was something which made the man act as he did.

"Or probably a Murdered Body, hidden somewhere," Meg continued.

"They're not criminals, Meg," Carolyn told her soberly. "They seemed nice, that day I met them. Something happened to them—I don't know what, but something must have happened. Mr. Warren wasn't angry like that the day I saw him on the caboose. He was just quiet and read a book all the time."

"He could have committed the murder since," Meg pointed out.

"Yes," Carolyn admitted. "But he didn't."

They rode on in silence. Presently, Meg spoke again.

"You can do as you like, Carolyn Pierce," she declared, "but I don't intend to tell anyone we went to the Warrens. It will be a sort of secret, and secrets are always fun."

Carolyn questioned whether that was her real reason for not telling. Neither Meg nor Carolyn, as far as that went, knew exactly how their mothers were going to react to the visit.

"Are you going to blab it to your mother, Carolyn?" Meg asked.

"Well—" Carolyn hesitated.

"Nobody told us not to go," Meg pointed out.

"They didn't know we gave it a thought," Carolyn reminded her.

"Anyway, I don't mean to tell. It will be lots more fun if we don't tell. Promise me you won't."

Carolyn hesitated. Meg was always wanting to have a "secret," something mysterious, something known only to the two of them. And there was really no reason why this story should be told. As far as Carolyn was concerned, the less she thought about the matter the better she would like it.

"I won't tell," she promised.

"Good!" Meg exclaimed. "My—but didn't we have a surprise?" She giggled delightedly, remembering the episode. "The way he said 'Go away' and shut that door right in our faces!"

Yes, that had been a surprise, all right. But it hadn't been the big one for the day. The real surprise had been the sight of Elizabeth, standing there telling Mr. Warren he ought to be ashamed of himself. She was every bit as scared as Meg or Carolyn, perhaps more so. But she was the one who had found her tongue and jumped in to defend her friend. That was like Katie—for herself she was timid, but when someone else needed her, Katie sailed in with a blind courage which took her beyond what ordinary people would think of doing. Maybe that was the best kind of courage to have—the sort which set you out to look after other people.

"Meg," Carolyn said, "you and I can talk all we want to, but don't forget it was Elizabeth who spoke up to him."

"That's right," Meg agreed. "My goodness, Elizabeth, you are the brave one! You've learned to ride a horse, and you squared off and told Mr. Warren what was what."

"I didn't want him fussing at Carolyn when we were as much to blame as she was," Elizabeth said. She spoke quietly, but her face was bright with pride and happiness.

That's like Katie, Carolyn thought again. Brave as a lion when she's looking after someone else.

"I'll tell you the one I feel sorry for," Elizabeth said. "It's the girl—Rowena, didn't you say her name was? First she's out here with no friends her own age. Then she must feel badly about the way her father acts. I hope you have a chance to see her some time, Carolyn, and tell her we really didn't mind what he said."

"She's a nice girl," Carolyn said. "She's smart and friendly and—well, nice."

"I'm sorry I talked to her father the way I did," Elizabeth went on contritely. "If you see her, tell her I didn't mean what I said. It was very rude of me."

"It wasn't any such thing," Meg broke in. "He was horrid. You did exactly right!"

Elizabeth smiled gently. "I'm not so sure," she said. "I can't help being a little ashamed."

"You don't need to be," Carolyn burst out. "We—Meg and I—we were the ones who were bound and determined to go. And when he fussed at us, you were the only one who had the courage to stand up to him. I think you're just wonderful."

The look on Elizabeth's face was a most rewarding thing to see. It told Carolyn that her guest was pleased and happy to be accepted. It told her, also, that when she herself started to school in Amarillo in the fall, she could be sure of at least one friend there.

SIX

ELIZABETH WAS GONE. Dennis and Melinda had come out for her in the automobile. Her going left a great blank in Carolyn's life. She could not have borne it, she was sure, had there not been the prospect of the magic lantern show at the church to fill in the emptiness. A missionary and his wife, recently returned from Africa, were going to show pictures of the country where they served. The ladies of the church had planned an ice cream supper before the show. Every bit of money would go to the missionary. That way, it wouldn't seem wrong to be having it on Sunday.

"I'll bet everyone in the neighborhood—every single one—will come," Meg said. "Aren't you excited, Carolyn?"

Mrs. Cartwright had come over to discuss the plans

with Mama, bringing Meg with her. The two women sat talking inside the house now, while Meg and Carolyn stayed out by the windmill for their own visiting.

As a matter of fact, Carolyn was. She was so excited she could scarcely sleep nights, thinking about all the delights in prospect. Imagine seeing a really-truly missionary who had been to darkest Africa and had returned alive. Out among savages he had been—and maybe even cannibals! In her mind's eye, she could see him, a man at least six feet tall, strong and handsome, perhaps with a halo around his head, showing the pictures of all the strange and amazing places he had seen with his own eyes —animals, and the small, dark men who peered at one from the pages of the geography book. Oh, it was all wonderful beyond telling!

And, as if the ice cream supper and the pictures were not enough, Mrs. Cartwright had worked up another idea. She had suggested that the ladies turn the whole program over to the young people, especially since the women would have their hands full with the supper. Accordingly, it had been arranged. Katie was going to sing. Meg would give a recitation (something deeply significant about a little black boy who insisted his soul was white). Carolyn would read the Scripture. Even the Adams boys would have a part (to keep them from pulling off some joke that would break up the meeting). They were going to pass the plate—to take up the collection.

"Yes," Meg said, "I'll bet just everybody will be there."

There was no arguing with that statement, Carolyn thought.

"Except," Meg went on, looking around her to be sure no one was listening, and even then speaking softly, although nobody was near, "except, the Warrens. Do you suppose they'll come?"

"I don't know," Carolyn said uncomfortably.

She couldn't quite explain the guilt she felt about their visit to the Warrens. Perhaps it was because Meg had built the episode up as a secret misdemeanor of theirs, something which they must hug close to themselves and never, never reveal. Actually, they hadn't done anything wrong. True, they had not been given permission to go see the Warrens, but then, they had not asked for it.

"You haven't told, have you?" Meg asked.

"No," Carolyn answered briefly.

Why hadn't she told Mama, Carolyn wondered. She should have told Meg she could not hold to her promise to keep it all a secret and gone home right away and told her about the sick woman, and Mama would have gone with soup and custards and kind offers of help. Why hadn't she told?

Was it because she was embarrassed by the whole thing? True, she had let Meg talk her into it, but actually, she had felt pretty sure herself that she would be received where others, her mother and Mrs. Cartwright included, had been turned away. Hadn't she already met the family and talked with them, especially with Rowena? Hadn't she given them cookies and other things to eat? Yes, she had been pretty confident that, once she announced herself, the door would swing open and all would be well.

But it hadn't. Instead, Mr. Warren had come to the door and spoken as no one had ever spoken to her before —with Meg and Elizabeth listening. Perhaps she hadn't told because it wouldn't make very pleasant telling. Her pride had been pricked.

"No," she said, "I haven't told—"

"Well, don't," Meg said importantly. "That way, we'll have a secret. Isn't it fun to have a real secret?"

Carolyn couldn't in the least agree with her, although she did not say so. She wasn't able to see anything that even resembled fun about the whole thing. She kept seeing Rowena's stricken face, kept hearing her words, "Oh, Papa—she's the one who gave us the cookies—"

There was, too, another memory. Elizabeth's words— "I'll tell you the one I feel sorry for. It's the girl . . . I hope you have a chance to see her . . ."

It was Rowena who deserved the sympathy. Carolyn wondered whether she would ever have another chance to see the girl and try to make her feel better about the whole thing. If the Warrens would only come to the magic lantern show, maybe Carolyn could find her chance. But she didn't look for them. Meg, for all her surmising, didn't expect them, either.

Now that the day of the magic lantern show had come at last and the Pierces were really there, Carolyn could see that, although the Warrens had not come, just about everyone else in the community had. Row after row of teams were lined up at the hitchracks. Horse after horse, saddled and bridled, stood beside them. Carolyn was impressed by the number. She didn't know whether to be glad because of all the money it would mean for the missionary or scared to think of having to read the Scripture before all those people.

Across the heads of the gathering crowd, Carolyn saw Meg and started making her way toward her friend.

"Oh, hello," Meg said, once they were together. "My, you look nice!"

"So do you," Carolyn replied. The two girls smoothed down their skirts and fluffed out their hair ribbons.

"I'm glad you wore your white dress. Mama said white was more appropriate."

"That's what my mama said, too. Let's walk around."

Together, they made their way across in the general direction of the food stand, where all the women were busily at work. Carolyn could see Mama, her dress protected by a long apron, helping get things organized. Freezers of ice cream, with the ice melting and making little pools of water around them; great jars of lemonade with half-lemons, squeezed free of juice, floating on the surface of the liquid; row after row of cakes—all these promises of delight were inside the food stand.

"I have my own money," Meg announced. "When it comes time to eat, let's go together. Do you have your money?'

"Of course," Carolyn said.

"Let's wait awhile, though. It's sort of fun to look forward to it, don't you think?"

"Oh, yes!" Carolyn agreed.

"Besides, I have something to tell you," Meg went on mysteriously.

Carolyn shifted uncomfortably from one foot to the other. She had had about enough of Meg's secrets!

"Do you want to hear it, or don't you?" Meg demanded with an injured air.

"Yes, I want to hear it," Carolyn assured her.

"Well, my mama thought it was wrong not to ask the Warrens to this magic lantern show, even if they hadn't been nice to her when she called, so she went over again, and do you know what happened?"

She paused, giving Carolyn ample time to wonder.

"They wouldn't even come to the door, that's what! She knocked and she knocked, and they didn't even come."

Carolyn wanted to tell Meg there was nothing strange about this. The Warrens had done exactly the same thing when her own mother tried to be friendly with them.

"It's just the way I told you," Meg continued triumphantly. "There's some Deep, Dark Mystery there. That's why they won't let anyone in. If anybody ever got inside the house, he'd see what it was. That's why the Warrens won't let visitors inside."

"Oh, nonsense, Meg!" Carolyn said, somewhat sharply. She had seen the Warrens. They weren't the sort of people who went in for mysteries. Something had happened, all right, but it wasn't a dark secret, the way Meg hinted. "Nonsense, Meg! You know that isn't so."

"I don't, and neither do you," Meg insisted stoutly. "And quit being so positive about it. Come on, let's get our ice cream and lemonade now. I can't wait any longer."

"All right," Carolyn agreed. She was glad to get her companion off the subject of the Warrens. Of course, Meg was all wrong about that mystery part. She loved pretending she found mysteries everywhere, without actually believing she had at all. But something had happened—something strange and unexplainable—to change the family Carolyn had met in the caboose into the kind of people they had now become—the kind Carolyn herself had seen them to be, the day she had knocked on the door of their dugout. In a way, Meg was right, though. There was some mystery there; or, at least, something that Carolyn did not in the least understand.

The ice cream, the cake and the lemonade were all just lovely memories now. The women at the stand were putting things in order, hurrying so as not to be late for the program. Mama handed Katie a basket.

"Here," she said, "take this to the carriage. And hurry, honey, because you want to slip inside ahead of the others and rest a minute, so you won't be all out of breath when it comes time for you to sing."

Katie, basket in hand, started toward the carriage, walking faster than she usually moved. At that moment, a group of children headed for the church, too, running like mad. You'd think they were afraid they'd never get in at all if they didn't go right this minute. One of them, flying past Katie and not watching where he was going, ran into her. With the heavy basket in her arms, Katie couldn't seem to get balanced. She would have fallen, sure as anything—if something hadn't happened.

Bryan Cartwright, talking to a group of men close by, saw Katie's predicament. He was at her side so fast it was almost as if a spring had been released inside him. He caught her, set her on her feet once more.

"Are you hurt?" he asked, as pale as if he had been the one who had come close to falling.

"No—" Katie told him. "Oh, no—"

Even though she was standing straight once more, he still held fast to her. Katie made no move to pull away— no move at all. She just stood there, very still, with Bryan's arm half around her, as it had been when he caught her from falling. Her cheeks were getting all pink and pretty again, the way they used to be. She looked at Bryan shyly, and he held on to her as if he never meant to let go—not ever.

"Katie!" Someone was calling her. "Katie—come quick! They want you to start playing the organ so people will know it's time to go into the church."

Bryan dropped his arm. He stepped back from her. Katie just stood there, looking as if she didn't want to play the organ at all, which was strange, for usually she'd rather play than eat.

Slowly, as if he were coming back from a great distance, Bryan spoke. "Go on and play the organ, Katie," he told her. "I'll put the basket in the carriage."

And, when she hesitated, he said, giving her a little push in the direction of the church, "Hurry—they're waiting for you."

He turned and walked toward the carriage. Katie watched him for a moment, then moved slowly off in the direction of the church. Oh, bother the music, Carolyn thought. The people would have gone in without it. If Bryan and Katie had been left alone another minute, they might have patched things up.

"Come on, Carolyn," Meg called. "It's time we went in. Mama says so."

When the two girls walked inside the church, Mrs. Cartwright was already up at the front. She motioned for them to come and join her. Katie was playing the organ softly. The missionary sat in one of the pulpit chairs. He was a little man, with a thoughtful look, as if

99

all the woes of those men and women in darkest Africa sat right on his shoulders.

"That's his wife, in the front seat," Meg whispered, so loudly that the woman must have heard her, for she half-turned to look in their direction.

She, too, was small. Her dress was old-fashioned and didn't fit too well. But still she looked serene and happy, as if stylish clothes weren't important at all compared with the good work she did.

"Guess who's going to lead the program," Meg said, apparently delighted that she should know these things. "Jim Foster. He drove the missionaries out in a livery-stable rig, so Mama thought he could just take charge, since this is a young people's program. My, isn't he the best-looking thing?"

"Yes," Carolyn agreed briefly.

Jim Foster was going to lead. He would be the one who would announce that she, Carolyn Pierce, would read the Scripture. Oh, why hadn't she practiced more? Mama had tried to get her to read that portion over and over, but she had insisted that she knew it all right. There wasn't a single word she couldn't pronounce, and what more could anyone ask? She had been a big silly to stand around outside, watching people and eating ice cream and drinking lemonade. She should have been in here half an hour ago, practicing. Where would she stand, anyway? Not in the pulpit, to be sure. Nobody but a preacher or a missionary or a superintendent of the Sunday School had a right to do that! Why hadn't she asked someone?

Everybody who could get inside the church was in now; the others were standing outside, looking in the

windows. Jim Foster glanced at Mrs. Cartwright, who
nodded to him. He stepped forward, right up into the
pulpit, as if he were the superintendent or somebody like
that. He seemed very much at ease and, as Meg had said,
very good-looking.

"We are awfully glad you have all come," he said. "We
think you will enjoy the program. The first number will
be Miss Katie Pierce, singing 'From Greenland's Icy
Mountains.' "

Mama moved forward to take her place at the organ
and struck the first notes. Katie began to sing.

> *From Greenland's icy mountains,*
> *From India's coral strand—*

Her voice rang out, clear and sweet, but sad. It made
Carolyn want to cry, listening to her.

> *Where Africa's sunny fountains,*
> *Roll down their golden sand—*

Africa's sunny fountains. They came before Carolyn
now, warm and bright and distant. Fountains flowing
among strange, dark people, unlike anyone she knew here.
People whose sad lot the missionary was going to describe. It wasn't their sadness Katie sang about, however, but her own. Bryan Cartwright, standing at an open
window and never taking his eyes off her, must have
realized that.

Carolyn, intent on Katie and the reason for her sadness,
heard someone calling her name. Jim Foster was announc-
ing, "And now Miss Carolyn Pierce will read the Scripture."

Miss Carolyn Pierce! The sound of it made a great

shyness come over her. She didn't think she could possibly walk up to the front; she knew she couldn't take even the first little step to cross that narrow space between the front seat, where she sat with Meg, to the pulpit, where Jim stood. She couldn't, with all those people watching her—friends and neighbors, her family—and Jim Foster, who had just called her "Miss." From somewhere in the back of her mind, a memory leaped out at her. She remembered herself telling Katie to hurry and get married so she, Carolyn, could be "Miss Pierce." How the twins had laughed at the prospect of eight-year-old Carolyn being "Miss." Would they laugh now, because when she actually was called "Miss," out in public, she couldn't walk forward and read the Scripture?

Across the distance between them, she could feel Jim Foster's eyes upon her. His lips shaped words and she could read them, plain as if he had said them aloud. "Come on, Carolyn," his look as well as his lips said. *"Come on!"*

It was his command, not any conscious effort on her part, which seemed to draw her forward. She came to the pulpit, stopped, uncertain where to go. The merest motion of his hand and he had directed her to a spot, inside the railing, in front and to one side of the pulpit. Carolyn stepped into place.

"Read," he whispered, so softly nobody else could possibly have heard. His eyes on hers were both commanding and kind—and, some way, full of courage which carried over to her.

She lifted the piece of paper on which she had written the portion of Scripture she was to read. She cleared her throat. No sound came. She tried again. Then, suddenly, she was speaking.

"For the Lord thy God bringeth thee into a good land," she heard herself saying. "A land of wheat and barley— a land where thou shalt eat bread without scarceness—"

Her voice went on, gaining strength and confidence. She read on to the end, then made her way back to her seat.

When she had finished, the missionary began praying, taking up the words she had read, enlarging upon them. He prayed that the Lord would make them thankful for this good land where they were living—it was, indeed, good. From the depths of dark Africa from which he came, he could assure the people here that this was the best of lands, and they should be grateful. In their gratitude, they must reach out to help those less fortunate—

Of course this is a good land, Carolyn thought. She felt a great wish to help somebody else, just to show how grateful she was because she had so many blessings. She could understand now why the missionary's wife didn't feel that new, fine clothes were necessary; she could see why the missionary would want to go to Africa and help the people there. Then another thought came to her.

Those new people, those Warrens—they wouldn't think so. To them, it must seem anything but good; otherwise, why would they shut themselves off from the people who lived here? Again, Rowena's face came before Carolyn, and she heard Elizabeth's words, "I hope you have a chance to see her—"

The missionary stopped praying and sat down. Jim, stepping forward once more, this time to announce Meg Cartwright's speech, looked straight at Carolyn. And when he did, he smiled, just the least little bit, but it was a smile—and it was meant for her!

All too soon it was over. The last pictures had flashed across before the eyes of the wondering people. The money had been counted (the Adams boys were as grave as judges and twice as careful when they took up the collection) and turned over to the missionary and his wife, who looked very happy.

"The Lord will bless you," they said together, "and this money which will be dedicated to His work."

And now, Papa was driving home. Katie and Carolyn, together in the back seat of the Pierce surrey, had little to say.

"It worked out well," Mama said. "I was proud of both of you—Katie, Carolyn."

"And so was I," Papa told them. "I was mighty proud of my girls."

"Thank you," Katie said listlessly.

"I thought I wasn't going to be able to read at all, there for a while," Carolyn admitted honestly.

"Oh," Mama assured her, "almost everyone feels that way, the first time he performs in public. You read well. I could understand every word."

If it hadn't been for Jim Foster I never would have started, Carolyn was thinking.

Mama must have sensed her thoughts. "Jim Foster did awfully well," Mama said. "I was proud of him. I wish Annie could have seen him."

Carolyn didn't answer her. She couldn't think of a thing to say.

Just at the edge of the sky, where it dipped down to

meet the land, the moon came bobbing up. Like a huge
globe, it was, and bright as a lamp burning. Beneath it,
the country stretched out, all washed in silver light. It
was so bright you could see the fields and the houses scattered here and there and stock grazing in the pastures.
A good land—she had read those words and the missionary
had repeated them in his prayers. *A good land.*

Carolyn turned to Katie to ask, "Isn't it pretty, Katie?
Like a picture—"

Only she didn't say a word, for, in the brightness of the
moonlight, she saw something that made her forget about
how pretty the moon was. Katie was crying—softly, so no
one could hear her, and trying to cover it up. But, all
the same, she was crying.

SEVEN

CAROLYN STOOD WATCHING the family surrey disappear in the distance. Little swirls of dust followed, but even so, she could see Mama and Katie sitting in the back seat and Papa in the front, driving the team. The sun was just coming up and there was a coolness in the air, one that promised fall would be there before too long. The morning had a fresh, clean look to it, a quality which made the girl glad to be alive. She was Carolyn Pierce, close to fifteen years old, and she was going to spend two days with her friend, Meg Cartwright, while Papa and Mama and Katie went to Amarillo. It had been her own decision not to accompany the family to town.

"You can go if you want to, Carolyn," Mama had pointed out to her. "You know you can."

"Of course," Carolyn told her, "I know it. But if I

stay home, there'll be more room in the surrey for all the things you need to bring back."

"Well—" Mama hesitated. "Yes, there will be, Carolyn," she admitted, "but if you want to go, we'll make room for you."

"There's no need," Carolyn said. She knew as well as anyone what these twice-a-year shopping trips meant— the family pretty well stock up on the basic supplies for the next six months. When the Pierces had first come out to the Panhandle, those trips were made in a wagon, but now Papa went in the surrey and brought back as much as he could. Later, the wagon would be sent in for the larger articles. "You can bring back a lot more if I don't go," the girl persisted. "Besides, I had my trip to Amarillo in June. It's Katie's turn, now."

"That's very thoughtful of you, Carolyn," Mama told her. "I know your sister appreciates it. Don't you, Katie?"

"Yes, Mama," Katie answered dutifully, not seeming to care much one way or another.

The surrey was only a speck in the distance—that long, infinite distance of the Texas Panhandle. Carolyn wondered what the three in that disappearing vehicle would say if they knew the real reason behind her decision to stay at home—if they had been given even a hint that she was about to undertake something for Katie's sake. Carolyn almost hugged herself with sheer joy at the prospect. When Katie came back, late tomorrow evening, she was going to find a wonderful gift waiting for her—one that Carolyn knew her sister wanted more than anything in the world.

She went to the barn where her horse stood, already

saddled and bridled. He gave a welcoming neigh as she came near, and she patted his neck. "Good boy," she said. "Good Prince." She placed her book sack, with her over-night supplies in it, over the saddle horn and then sprang into the saddle and rode away, taking one backward glance at the house.

Funny how sad and lonesome an empty house looked— like a person left by himself when everyone else was off having a good time. Wouldn't it be nice if a house could go along, too? Carolyn almost hated to leave it with the windmill creaking lonesomely and the chickens raising a fuss in the chicken yard, trying to tell the world how glad they were that a new day had come—almost as if they themselves had brought it.

Carolyn rode on slowly toward the Catrwrights'. Now that she was on her way, she was a little frightened. How was she going to set about accomplishing her errand, any-way? She had thought that, just by being at the Cart-wrights' for two days, she would work out everything as easy as could be. But how? Meg would be with her every minute, every single minute. And her friend had eyes as sharp as a hawk's, and the curiosity of a magpie. Not that Carolyn had ever seen a magpie, but the books said they were very curious. If Carolyn made a move—even the beginnings of a move—to carry out what she had in mind, Meg would catch on and want to know all about it. Oh, dear, Carolyn thought, wasn't I stupid not to think of that before? She turned the problem over and over in her mind. But try as she would, she couldn't think, off hand, of a sure way of getting Bryan off by himself, so she could ask him why he acted as he did toward Katie; so she could tell him Katie felt terribly sad because he didn't come to see her any more.

Well, she had two whole days. She would watch for every possible chance and surely before she left she would find some way to work things out.

Of course, she had not really expected she would have a chance to talk to Bryan right away. When he came in for dinner the first day of her visit he seemed a little surprised to see her, but he was nice enough.

"Hello, young'un. What are you doing here? Your folks run you away from home?" he teased.

"What a way to talk," Mrs. Cartwright protested. "She's here while her folks are in Amarillo, buying supplies. Now sit down and start eating. I fried chicken for you."

Mrs. Cartwright spoiled Bryan outrageously. You'd think he was a baby, not able to feed himself at all, the way she acted. She searched the plate of chicken, hunting for his favorite piece, and when she located it, she put it on his plate.

"Thanks," he said, grinning at her. He took a bite, his teeth showing white and strong in his tanned face. His eyes crinkled up a little. "Sun grins," his mother called them, and said it was because he was outside so much.

"You wouldn't want me cooped up inside, like a sick kitten, would you?" he had teased her.

"Mr. and Mrs. Pierce and Katie went," Meg put in importantly. "They are also going to attend the musical program at the Opera House while they are there. Carolyn did not want to go. She is not cultured, like Katie."

Bryan laid down his fork. "Excuse me, Mama," he said.

"I think I'd better be getting back to work. I want to finish that fence this afternoon."

"You haven't eaten all your chicken," his mother worried.

"I've had all I want," he told her. And then he was up and away.

Carolyn watched him leave in a troubled frame of mind. It was the mention of Katie that had done it. He didn't want to finish his meal, once he heard her name. Maybe he wouldn't listen to her at all, when he found out what she wanted to talk about, Carolyn thought despairingly. Maybe she wasn't going to get anywhere, even if she had a chance to shake off Meg, which didn't seem likely at the minute.

It was mid-afternoon of the second day of the visit. Sure enough, Meg had been at Carolyn's side every second of the time. There had been paper dolls to cut out and a bout at cooky making and long rides. There had been much giggling and talking after the girls went to bed, until Mr. Cartwright knocked smartly on the wall between the two rooms, a sign indicating that it was time to go to sleep, and no more nonsense. But there had been no chance at all to talk to Bryan alone.

Now, out of desperation, a plan had come to Carolyn.

"I'm going home and get things ready for the family," she told Mrs. Cartwright.

"What if they come home late?" Mrs. Cartwright worried. "I shouldn't let you go, Carolyn."

"They said they'd be home early," Carolyn replied. "Besides, Dick and Bert will be over, doing the milking and looking after the stock. I won't be alone."

That made sense, so Mrs. Cartwright consented to let
her leave. She and Meg both called after Carolyn as long
as they thought she could hear, and then went on waving
to her. Out here in this country, company was something
special. You loved having guests come; you hated seeing
them go. Once more, Carolyn thought of the Warrens,
who had shut themselves off from their own kind. It was
an act past understanding. People were meant to stick
together. If you didn't need others, there was always the
chance that they would need you. You had no right to
withdraw from your neighbors.

The girl pushed the Warrens out of her thoughts. She
had other business on hand. She was going to circle the
field where Bryan was making fence. She would talk with
him and then, once she had finished, she would double
back toward home.

Carolyn saw him a long way off, working on the fence.
His horse was tied to a post; his hat was on the back of
his head. She could hear the sound of his hammer now
and then; and, between times, she could see him walking
along to inspect more of the fence.

"Oh, hello," he said, looking up as she rode close to
him. "On your way home?"

"Yes," Carolyn told him.

Here she was, where she had wanted to be—alone with
Bryan—and she didn't know what to do! All the speech
she had memorized (even saying it out loud to herself
once, just to be sure she had it well planned) refused to
come off her tongue. That fine speech which was going
to set things straight between Katie and Bryan remained
undelivered! It was a dozen times worse than the day

she had almost failed to read the Scripture—that would have meant only embarrassment, had she failed. This was different. Katie's happiness—and maybe Bryan's as well—rested in this moment.

Bryan selected a staple, drove it into the post. No wonder Katie liked him. Those "sun grin" wrinkles made a pattern of kindness and fun on his face. He could laugh at a lot of things—and often did so. He was smart, too. Papa said he was a born farmer; he seemed to know by instinct how to manage land. His one dream was to be able to buy a section of land for himself.

"That's a nice fence you're making," Carolyn remarked, trying to fill in time, trying to act as if it were the most natural thing in the world for her to ride out of her way to get from the Cartwright place to her own home.

"Glad you like it," Bryan said. He sounded a little as if he were laughing at her, but in a kind sort of way.

"My papa said you do everything you undertake well," she went on.

"Oh, he did—" Bryan was really laughing at her now. "That's nice of him." His voice had taken on a hint of mockery.

"He certainly did say that." Carolyn felt her temper coming up. "And you needn't act as if he didn't mean it. He said you were a good farmer, and he knows."

Bryan had no reason to laugh at her. When the Pierces first came out here, there wasn't another farmer around except the Fosters, and the ranchers had called them nesters and didn't want them. Now, lots of people were buying land here and the ranchers, she supposed, had either given up objecting or had realized it was no use.

By the time the Cartwrights came, things were easier.
Who was Bryan Cartwright to laugh at *her?*

"My papa says you have a real future," Carolyn declared, holding her ground.

"On the farm," Bryan said flatly. "A future on the
farm."

"What's wrong with that?" she demanded hotly. "Papa
and the twins are farmers. They like it. All of us do.
We belong here."

"Not your sister Katie," Bryan corrected her, looking
as if he were biting down on on aching tooth. "She
doesn't—"

"She does, too!"

Here it was, her chance. Bryan himself had brought up
Katie's name. He didn't look in the mood to listen to
anything she would say, but still, she had him alone, and
he had mentioned Katie.

"You are rude to Katie," Carolyn told him. She felt
very young as she spoke, and hopeless and helpless. But
she had started, and she was going to finish. "She is sad
because you are so rude. You won't look at her, or come
to see her, or talk to her, or anything—" Her voice trailed
off.

Bryan laid down his hammer. He looked Carolyn
straight in the eye, and now he was not laughing.

"See here, Carolyn," he began. "You're old enough
to listen to sense. Nobody else will, but maybe I can
make you see it. Katie's not a farm girl. She's all wrapped
up in music and painting and singing—things that don't
belong on a farm at all. A girl who can do those things
doesn't belong on a farm, either. She might think she
does, or might be sweet and kind enough to want others to

think she does. But it would be—well, it would be a prison to her. You understand?"

Carolyn shook her head. "No," she said.

"Oh, yes you do," he told her. "You understand perfectly."

Well, maybe she did—a little. Only, he was wrong. Wrong as he could be. "Katie was brought up on a farm," Carolyn reminded him. "She can do things like cooking and keeping house and so on. When Mama went back to East Texas, to look after Grandmother, Katie took care of us all—cooked and everything."

"Yes, I remember," Bryan said. "I came over once when she was cooking and doctored her burn. I put soda on it. Just because she can do it doesn't mean she should be made to go on cooking—and burning her hands—all her life. She needs someone to make things easy for her, to take care of her."

"She can take care of other people, too," Carolyn went on. "You remember how she looked after us when we were caught in the schoolhouse during the big snowstorm. She saved our lives."

"Yes," Bryan agreed, "she had to, and she did it. And as soon as that was over, she went back where she belonged, where she didn't have to cook and fight snowstorms. She went to school in East Texas, to learn to be a lady."

"Katie was always a lady," Carolyn told him hotly. "She did not have to go away to school in order to learn how to be one."

"That's what I mean," Bryan said, reaching for another staple and turning once more to the fence he had been mending. "Now, get along, young'un. You don't want dark to catch you on the road."

He gave the staple a smart rap, the gesture seeming to indicate that the conversation was finished and that's all there was to it. Carolyn sat there on her horse uncertainly for a moment or two, then rode off.

So this was the gift she was going to take back to Katie! All her scheming, all her planning—nothing had worked. Nothing had come of her efforts and her fine dreams.

Nothing at all.

"Carolyn—" Across the short distance between them, she heard Bryan calling her. She stopped, half-turned around, a wild hope rising within her that perhaps he had relented and would, after all, send a message to Katie— one that would make her sister turn bright and happy once more, the way she used to be.

"Carolyn," he said, "you're a nice child and mighty smart for your age, but stop trying to mess around in grown-up stuff. It's like those big words you used to use— not quite your size yet!"

She did not even answer him. Instead, she gave Prince a quick slap of the reins and off they went down the road, faster than she had ever ridden before. She couldn't get away from Bryan Cartwright quickly enough. *Stop trying to mess around in grown-up stuff.* He had been half-laughing when he said it. *It's like those big words you used to use.*

Bryan Cartwright was the most hateful person she knew! Katie was lucky to be rid of him.

Her disgust with Bryan held Carolyn so completely that she was almost past the Warren place before she knew it. In fact, it was not until she was close to the little creek that she noticed it, sitting alone and dejected, like the people who lived there. Prince's feet were almost on the bridge when someone appeared so suddenly from behind the trees growing beside the stream that the horse shied at the sight of her. Carolyn, reining her mount in quickly, saw with surprise that it was Rowena.

"Hello—" the girl said breathlessly.

"Hello," Carolyn answered warily. Mr. Warren might be hidden behind those trees. He could pop out any minute and order Carolyn to ride on.

"Can you—can you stop a minute?" Rowena asked diffidently. Carolyn could see that her cheeks were red with embarrassment, and her eyes had a begging look to them.

Carolyn stopped, but made no move to get off her horse. Rowena walked closer and put out her hand, to grasp Prince's bridle in order to be sure Carolyn would not leave. Then, apparently thinking better of this, she dropped her hand to her side.

"I want to tell you—" the girl began. "I mean—I have to say something to you. I'm sorry. I mean— I feel simply terrible about the way my father acted. That day you came to see us—after you had been so nice to us and all—" Much as she wanted to say those words, she was obviously not finding it easy.

"Oh, that's all right," Carolyn assured her warmly.

"Oh, no, it isn't. It was awful. I felt dreadful. So did Van, and so did Mama, when she found out it had been you. She cried—"

"She shouldn't—" Carolyn broke in.

"Well, she did. And I did, too. And then she and I

talked about it and she said, if I ever had a chance, I should try to apologize to you."

"You needn't—" Carolyn said.

"Ever since that day," Rowena went on, "I have been hoping I'd have a chance to tell you. I wished I would get to see you—I wished *so* hard. And when I saw you come riding down the road just now, I knew my wish was coming true, so I ran—my, I ran fast—to stop you here."

She had run here because, from here, nobody could see her—Carolyn corrected her thoughts—her father couldn't see her. Perhaps her mother had even sent her. At that moment, a voice called.

"Rowena! Where are you?"

"That's Papa, calling me," the girl said. "It's time for me to get supper. I cook, now that Mama hasn't been so well—"

"Rowena!" the voice called again.

"I must go," she said, "and I haven't even had a chance to talk to you." Her eyes were enormous in her small face. "Listen," she went on desperately, "I have to talk to you. I just have to—"

"Well—" Carolyn began. If Rowena wanted to talk, why didn't she come over to the Pierce place, like any other girl would? But, even as the thought occurred to her, she knew it was useless. Mr. Warren wouldn't let his daughter go. For some reason Carolyn did not know, the man was determined to shut his family off from everyone—even from Carolyn, whom he had seemed at least to accept, that day in the caboose.

"You'll come back, won't you?" Rowena spoke urgently.

Carolyn hesitated.

"I come here every afternoon to read. Papa thinks it's

fine for me to read. And if I'm here and you ride by, it's all right, isn't it? I mean, I can't tell you not to ride down this road. I mean—we could talk, that way. And I *have* to talk to you. You will come back, won't you?" Rowena was almost crying in her great eagerness to have Carolyn promise.

"Rowena!"

The voice was louder now, more insistent.

"Promise?" Rowena begged, turning to hurry toward the house. "Oh, do promise me you'll come!"

I hope you'll have a chance to see her, Carolyn—Elizabeth's words came back.

"Yes," Carolyn said, "I'll come. If I can manage, I'll meet you here. The first afternoon I can get here, I'll come."

"Oh, thank you—thank you, Carolyn Pierce," Rowena cried. She didn't look frightened now, or unhappy or sad. She looked like any other girl her age whose friend had just promised to visit her. "Thank you," she said again—and started running toward the house.

Carolyn rode off. She slapped the reins across Prince's neck. She had better ride fast if she wanted to be home before the family. Even so, she slowed down for one more look. The Warren dugout sat, alone and lonely, a small bump on the prairie. Rowena was nowhere to be seen. She had evidently gone inside to start supper, as her father had wanted her to do. Even so, Carolyn could still see, in her mind, the girl's glowing face when she had been given the promise of another visit. The remembrance almost pushed aside the anger and humiliation Carolyn had experienced in her encounter with Bryan Cartwright— almost, but not quite.

EIGHT

"AND THAT'S THE REASON back of it, Carolyn," Rowena was saying. "That's why Papa acts the way he does—"

Carolyn and Rowena were sitting together, down by the little creek which ran through the Warren place. The trees hid them from the house—and from Mr. Warren, who was cutting lake hay on the other side of the farm.

"Mowing's hard for him to do," Rowena had explained. "He just doesn't know the first thing about farming. But that hay will be good for the cow."

"Oh, of course," Carolyn agreed. "Papa says it's awfully good for cows."

It was good for cows—but it was also the reason for Mr. Warren's being out of the way, which made it possible for the girls to have a visit without interference. It had given

Rowena a chance to tell Carolyn a lot of things during this, their first visit together. It was surprising how much Carolyn had found out about the Warren family in this short time. Rowena had spilled out the story, as if she couldn't talk long enough or fast enough, now that the chance had come at last.

Mr. Warren had owned a store back in Chicago—a small store, but even so, it might have done all right, had Mr. Warren not taken in a partner. He knew the man well and thought he could trust him. But, the way things turned out, the partner was a bad man.

"He put Papa's name on notes, Carolyn, and Papa had to pay them. Oh, it was awful!"

Then, as if that wasn't enough bad luck, Mrs. Warren became ill.

"The doctor said she ought to come out West," Rowena told her visitor, "and while we were wondering how we could manage, a friend said he knew about some land that could be bought cheap, out in the Texas Panhandle. He was a real-estate man, and he was Papa's friend, and he advised Papa to sell what interest he had left in the store—the notes and things had taken most of it—and buy this place he knew about."

So Mr. Warren had taken the advice of his friend and had bought the land. The friend said it had a house on it—and a well. And he said the land was good—the best. So Mr. Warren had taken what money he had left and bought the farm, without ever seeing it himself, all on the advice of this real-estate friend of his. The family packed their things and started to the Panhandle.

"We traveled in what the railroad called an immigrant

car," Rowena explained. "That way we could watch our things."

"I know," Carolyn said. "Lots of people are coming in on them these days."

"They are?" Rowena asked. "Papa thought maybe we were the only ones who had to do things that way."

"Well, you aren't," Carolyn assured her.

"We had the awfulest time getting here," Rowena went on. "Somewhere up the line—I think it was in Oklahoma —something happened. I don't know what, but we just sat there. It took us the longest time to get across one stretch. All the lunch Mama had packed was gone, and we were hungry. Finally, we came to a town, but we were afraid to buy very much because Papa had such a little bit of money."

She stopped, as if she were reliving that bitter memory all over again.

"At Amarillo, the conductor let us ride in the caboose. Then you got on. You were kind and friendly and you gave us something to eat. Oh, Carolyn, I can still remember how good that food tasted!"

A memory came back to Carolyn—Van, eating those cookies and the other food as if he were starved; Mrs. Warren giving her cooky to him. She wished, suddenly, that Melinda had seen fit to pack whole baskets of food that day, instead of just that little bit of lunch and the box of cookies for her father.

"Then, finally, we got here—to this place," Rowena went on with her account. "That was when the real shock came, when we saw the house! It was just a hole in the ground, Carolyn. Like a cellar, back home! The roof was going to pieces, and the windows—there were just two, one on each side—were broken. And dirty—oh, it was dirty! Mama was sick and didn't feel much like cleaning up, so Papa and Van and I did the best we could. But try as we would, we couldn't make it look like much."

Carolyn understood that. The mother of a family was the only one who could get a house looking really right. Maybe even Mrs. Pierce couldn't do much with the Warren place.

"It had dirt floors, Carolyn," Rowena said. "Did you ever hear of such a thing?"

"Why of course, Rowena," Carolyn told her. Memory stirred within her. "When we first came out here, we lived in a dugout and it had dirt floors—until Papa put some wooden ones in. We still use that dugout for Katie and me and the guest room, although it has been fixed up a lot."

"You do?" Rowena marveled.

"We certainly do," Carolyn assured her. "You needn't feel it isn't all right to live in a dugout."

"It wasn't just that," Rowena went on. "It was the farm itself. I don't quite know how to tell you this, but back where we came from, a place the size we bought seemed a mighty big farm, really enormous. A half-section—just rich people had that much land in Illinois. And when we got here, we found it wasn't much at all. Everyone has lots bigger places. It hurt Papa's pride terribly to have been taken in that way—and most of all because he had brought poor, sick Mama to such a shabby, run-down place with no improvements and not even a store near to fall back on."

We are going to be rich—Carolyn could hear Rowena's words, spoken with pride and hope, that day in the caboose. She could see how it would be hard to think you were going to have so much and find so little. And yet, the Warrens really did have something.

"You have a well and a windmill," Carolyn pointed out. "That's more than we had when we first came."

As, indeed, it was. Papa and the boys had hitched up a team to the wagon and had gone to the Kennedy Ranch for water. The Pierces had to be saving with every drop, every cupful of water, because it was so hard to come by. How much it had meant to all of them when they finally got the well and the windmill—not just the water alone, but the fact that they no longer must ask for it! Now it was theirs for free—the wind blew and turned the windmill which pumped the water. Papa had worked all one summer with the well diggers in order to get them to dig his own well. Melinda gave up her chance to go to East Texas to school when she found out that Papa was going to take money in payment for his work, instead of the well, so she could go there. Of course, Melinda really hadn't wanted to leave the Panhandle at all, but, even if she had, she would have given up school in favor of a well. That's the way you felt about water, out here in this country.

"You have a well and a windmill," Carolyn repeated firmly. "And you have this little creek and some trees. Rowena, you got a *lot* for your money!"

"I can see it, now that you tell me," Rowena said. "And anyway, I sort of like it here. Mama is beginning to feel better. And now that you have come to see me, I know I have a friend, so I'm really liking it. I needed a friend. We all do. Papa would like things better, I know, if he felt he had some friends out here—"

Carolyn wanted to remind her that it was his own fault he didn't have any friends. People had tried to be nice, and he had run them off. Rowena seemed to read her thoughts.

"I think he is ashamed to let people see how dreadful the house looks inside," Rowena said. "We had a nice place in Chicago—not big or fine, but nice, with a yard and trees and flowers and lots and lots of books. Oh, it was nice! But we lost it when we lost the store. I mean, we had to sell it, and Papa used the money to pay off those notes his bad partner had signed. . . . He really has had lots of reasons for being cross. I only wish that you could have known him back home. He was always so pleasant until the trouble began piling up. He wouldn't have talked crossly or rudely to a fly, even if it landed right on his nose!"

"We didn't have money either," Carolyn told her. "Not when we came out here, we didn't. I can remember— there was a fire back home and it burned Papa's store. He had just a little bit of money left, so he used it to make a payment on a place out here. Rowena, we were a lot like you are now!"

"You were?" Rowena asked incredulously. "I wish I could tell Papa that. He thinks you people are so rich you'd never understand what it means to have hard luck and be poor, the way we are. He says you'd laugh at us—"

"That's silly," Carolyn declared. "I mean—well, it's just silly to say such things. People out here aren't like that. They don't make fun of anybody for being poor."

"You're wrong there," Rowena corrected her. "They may not make fun of *you*, because you know them. But

they did make a fool out of Papa, right at the first, and
he can't seem to forget about it. I mean, about that dead
man—"

That joke the Adams boys had played on Mr. Warren!
That's what Rowena meant, Carolyn decided.

"Two boys said there was a dead man out at the corner
of the field and he went out and looked. It was night
and raining hard, but he got a lantern and he really
looked. And there wasn't any man at all, dead or not
dead. They were just making fun of him because he was
new. It was a cruel thing to do—especially when Papa
caught a dreadful cold and he was afraid that he would
give it to Mama."

"Oh, that," Carolyn said. "The Adams boys were the
ones. They are always playing jokes on people. They
don't mean any harm. It's just their idea of fun."

"Papa couldn't see it that way," Rowena said. "Piled
on top of everything else that had happened—the hard trip
down and the way the house looked and all—well, he just
couldn't take it. He felt that everyone who came might
be trying to make a fool out of him again, so he just
wouldn't let anyone come in. It was wrong of him, I
know, but there was no doing anything with him."

"Anyway," Carolyn told her, "there really was a 'dead
man' out there."

Rowena looked her unbelief.

"That's what they call a brace that holds a corner fence
post," Carolyn explained. "You do have one in the corner of your field. I saw it when I rode past today."

"Well, of all things!" Rowena marveled. "I'd like to
tell Papa that, but we just don't mention those two words

to him now. Maybe some day, when he sort of gets over being hurt—"

Mr. Warren was terribly hurt. That explained his strange actions. Of course, it wasn't right for him to judge a whole community by those two Adams boys who played thoughtless jokes on everyone. Yet how was he to know they weren't like the other neighbors? Hurt as he was, he was just ready to fly off the handle when the least little thing happened. In a way, Carolyn could understand him. It was sort of like being the baby of the family. When you finally lost your temper, it wasn't just because of what had happened at the moment; it was more likely to be a whole accumulation, like being teased and laughed at and left out of things the older ones did and made to feel you didn't know as much as they did. Mr. Warren felt left out and alone, here in this new, strange country.

"Well, anyway, that's how it all happened," Rowena was saying. "It's fine for me, now that I have a friend. You will come back to see me, won't you?"

Carolyn hesitated. She didn't know why she hadn't mentioned to her mother where she was going when she left home today. She had simply said, "I'm going riding, Mama," which she was.

Mama had looked up to say absently, "Well, don't go too far or stay too long."

She hadn't asked, "Where are you going?" If she had, Carolyn would have told her in a minute. Or would she? Mama wouldn't have minded her coming had she known how lonely Rowena was. But Mama hadn't asked, and Carolyn hadn't told her. And now here she was, sitting in the shade of the trees, down in the creek bed, hidden from the Warren house. Actually, it was a little like cheating. Why hadn't she told Mama where she was going?

Could it be because she was really a little like Meg in that she liked to have a secret? She might as well face it—this morning she had wakened with a feeling of great excitement, knowing she was going to ride over and meet Rowena. Because she meant to keep it a secret, the trip had a flavor which no ordinary visit could achieve. It somehow made her feel important—not just the baby of the family, tagging along behind one of the others, with no plans of her own. She could help Rowena—even if she had failed to fix things up for Katie.

"You will come, won't you?" Rowena was repeating. "Carolyn Pierce, I would simply *die* if you didn't come back, now that I know how wonderful it is to have you!"

"Yes," Carolyn promised. "I'll come. Maybe tomorrow. If not, the day after. But I'll come."

She couldn't bear not to promise. The look on Rowena's face reminded her of nothing so much as the way Van had looked that day he ate the cookies.

"I'll come," Carolyn assured her new friend once more. "Good-by for now, Rowena."

"Carolyn," Mama demanded, an edge of exasperation in her voice, "you must stop wiggling so I can get this hem even on your dress."

It would have been easy enough to say, "I can't stand still, Mama. I told Rowena I would come this afternoon, and I'm late already."

But she didn't say that. She didn't say anything at all, because, if she did, she'd have to go back and explain about that first time, when Mr. Warren had told the three girls to go away. To that, Mama would have just one reply: "Why didn't you tell me as soon as it happened?" And Carolyn did not know how she would answer the question.

She should have told Mama right away, and that was the truth. But she hadn't, and, because of the omission, she had been reluctant to tell about her chance encounter with Rowena. And, since she hadn't confided in Mama about that, she couldn't very well tell of the visits which followed. Once you started to deceive, no matter how innocently or accidentally, it sort of piled up on you, like a snowball rolling down hill, Carolyn thought uncomfortably.

"Do you think it's about right, Katie?" Mama asked now.

"Yes," Katie answered briefly.

Time was when Katie would have looked closely, her head on one side, the better to check. Katie had a way with sewing. But now she didn't seem especially interested in it—or in anything else, as far as that went. She was still feeling sad about Bryan. Carolyn wanted to tell her she wasn't losing anything. Bryan Cartwright was rude and ill-tempered. Katie was lucky to be rid of him. Only, of course Carolyn couldn't tell her sister this without going into the sources of her information, which, naturally, she couldn't do. It seemed as if her life was just one big secret after another!

"Well," Mama said, getting to her feet, "when I finish this I'll have the last of the sewing done. It's a good thing—we don't have too much time."

We don't have too much time! Her words went ringing through Carolyn's mind. Mama was thinking about sewing, but Carolyn was conscious only of the fact that she was going to be leaving to go to school in Amarillo in two weeks, and, as yet, she hadn't told Rowena. She must do it today, without fail. She couldn't just walk off and leave her new-found friend. Nor could she wait until the last minute. This would be a cowardly thing to do. She had waited too long, as it was.

"And that's it, Rowena," Carolyn said. "I'm going to high school in Amarillo. I won't be coming here to meet you much longer."

Rowena sat perfectly still, saying nothing.

"In about two weeks," Carolyn went on.

Still Rowena didn't answer. What was the matter? Didn't she understand? Or didn't she care? Carolyn cleared her throat. Maybe the girl hadn't heard her, and she ought to tell her once more.

Then Rowena broke the silence.

"I knew it had to stop. It was too good to be true. But I wouldn't let myself think about the stopping part. I'd just keep telling myself it was so wonderful to have you, I mustn't let my mind get off that. And it *was* wonderful. I was just about at the end of my rope, Carolyn Pierce, when I stopped you that day. You'll never know how you have helped me."

Carolyn wanted to answer, but there was a curious tightness in her throat which kept the words back.

"But if this is the last, it's the last," Rowena said staunchly, "and I can't let myself cry about it."

Her words were much braver than her heart. She was working at trying to keep from crying, but there were tears in her eyes and the muscles in her throat, Carolyn noticed, were jumping up and down. Brave—that was Rowena Warren—brave as could be. And suddenly Carolyn felt herself to be the weak one, the one who couldn't face the fact that this might be the last visit they would have. There was so much to do before she left.

"I tell you what, Rowena," Carolyn suggested, "why don't we both come back here tomorrow and have a—a sort of picnic? I'll bring some cookies and some apples— we have a tree ripe now."

Her voice trailed off, even as she tried to think of the things she would be able to get without telling her mother —and hating herself for the necessary deception.

"A picnic!" Rowena's face was glowing. "Oh, Carolyn, I haven't been to a picnic since we left Chicago! I'll bring something, too. I don't know what, but I'll bring something. We'll make it special—" She stopped abruptly. "You're sure you can manage to come?" she asked.

"I'm sure," Carolyn told her.

And she was. There was nothing that was going to keep her from this last visit with Rowena.

It all worked out better than Carolyn could have hoped for. She told Mama she was going riding, which she was, and Mama said, all by herself, "Do you want to take a lunch with you, Carolyn?" Somehow, Carolyn knew Mama was thinking the same thing she was—there wouldn't be too many times left when she could ride Prince off across the plains, taking her lunch with her— not too many times. Something like homesickness caught at her, which was a funny thing to have happen, standing here in the middle of the kitchen floor of her own home with her own mother speaking to her.

"Yes, Mama," Carolyn answered, feeling uncomfortable about the whole matter.

"Well," Mama suggested, "fix whatever you want. There are cookies and some fresh bread. And the apples are ripe."

Carolyn wound up with sandwiches made from Mama's bread and spread with butter churned only this morning; with cookies, still warm from the oven; and apples, picked off the tree by the windmill. It was a real feast.

"Have a good time," Mama called after her as she rode off. "Don't stay too late."

"All right," Carolyn promised.

She wouldn't listen to her conscience nagging at her, preferring, rather, to dwell on how pleased Rowena was going to be, once she got there.

Rowena was, indeed, delighted to see her.

"You came, Carolyn," she kept saying. "You *did* come."

"I told you I would," Carolyn reminded her.

"Yes, I know you did. But I told myself not to hope too much. Something could happen to keep you away. But now you are here!"

She let out her breath in a great sigh of happiness.

"Yes, I'm here," Carolyn said, feeling a quick sting of tears close behind her lids—and a relief, too, in the nagging little spot where her conscience had been troubling her. Oh, it was good she had come! It was *right* for her to have come.

"Guess what I have," Rowena cried, happiness spilling into her voice. Why she's really pretty, Carolyn thought.

When she's happy, the way she ought to be, she's one of the prettiest girls I know!

"I have some eggs," Rowena went on. "I got them honestly, too. I told Papa I was going to fix a lunch for myself, up here where I come to read, and he said that was all right. He doesn't care what I do, so long as I keep on reading," Rowena finished practically.

"I have cookies and sandwiches and apples," Carolyn told her, not mentioning her method—"honest" or otherwise—of coming by them.

"Now that's just perfect," Rowena marveled. "Those sandwiches, I mean, because I brought matches and some salt, and I'm going to build a campfire and roast those eggs."

Build a campfire! Doubt struck Carolyn. That was the one thing she had been taught not to do—all the people out here were taught the dangers of fire. A spark could get away from your campfire, easy as anything, and then a fire could be started and that was the worst thing that could happen—worse than blizzards or droughts or storms or anything. Once a fire started, nothing was safe—stock, or crops, or grass, or even human beings. She opened her mouth to tell Rowena she mustn't risk building a fire, not for anything.

"We always used to do this when we had a picnic back in Chicago," Rowena said. "Oh, Carolyn, I haven't had such a good time since I came out here!"

Carolyn's protest died on her lips. She couldn't tell Rowena, glowing with happiness as she was, that she mustn't do the very thing which was the cause of her happiness. Suddenly, Carolyn remembered the story the others often told (she had been asleep when it happened, so all of her knowledge was second-hand) about the time Dennis broke his leg and Melinda and Bert found him and built a fire out on the prairie, to guide the cowboys to where he lay. Of course, Melinda knew it was dangerous but, as she pointed out, it was an emergency. Besides, she and Bert watched it carefully, beating out any sparks which got out of hand.

Maybe this is an emergency, too, Carolyn thought. And, anyway, we'll watch carefully and be sure to put it out before we leave.

"I'll build it right down here in the creek bed," Rowena went on, proving that she, also, knew a thing or two about the dangers of campfires. "That way, it can't spread."

"Won't your father see the smoke?" Carolyn asked, still thinking there was a chance to put a stop to the whole enterprise.

"What if he does," Rowena answered easily. "I *told* him I was going to cook these eggs."

Even as she spoke, she raked a few twigs together and set a match to them. The flame rose, clear and steady, down in the dry creek bed. Rowena put on a few larger sticks. They caught, and soon a good little fire was burning. The girl's face was serene, carefree. She was in the clear, all right. She didn't have a thing in the world to worry about. Carolyn wished her own conscience could be equally as clear.

The eggs turned out very well—a little scorched, to be sure, but what else did one expect of eggs cooked in the ashes? Eaten with the sandwiches and followed by cookies and apples, they promised a feast. And, besides the food, there were a lot of things to talk about.

"You are mighty lucky, Carolyn Pierce," Rowena told her visitor, "to be going to school and all—"

"Well," Carolyn said, taking a bite of egg, "you'll be going, too, won't you?"

Rowena hesitated a little, flushed slightly, then went on bravely. "No," she answered finally, "no—I don't believe I will—"

She looked at Carolyn with a great hope in her eyes, a hope that her friend would understand why this must be.

"My goodness!" Carolyn burst out, ignoring the plea in her friend's look. "Everyone goes to school. And we've got a good teacher coming this year. Papa says she is one of the best. You're close enough to walk. Your Papa *has* to send you to school—"

"Papa says he is going to teach Van and me himself," Rowena went on steadily. "I know that's a funny way to do things, but he says he's going to. My father's real smart," she finished proudly.

"It's not so funny," Carolyn assured her. "When we first came out here, Mama taught Melinda and Katie and the twins. I was too little, but she had school for them five days a week, just like regular school."

"She did?" Rowena marveled.

"She certainly did," Carolyn assured her.

No need to add that, as soon as a real school opened up, Mama sent them all to it, every single day.

"Well," Rowena said, "I feel better about it now. But I'm disappointed. I had thought how much fun it would be to see all those children every day, if I went to school.

It would have been heaven!" She sighed as she said it. "But," she went on brightly, "I just mustn't let myself think about it. Besides, there probably isn't anyone I'd like as well as I do you, anyway."

"Nonsense!" Carolyn protested, pleased and touched. "There'd be lots of girls you'd like as well, or better—"

"Carolyn Pierce," Rowena declared firmly, "there won't ever be anyone as nice as you, anywhere, and you know it. It's all I can do to stand having you leave. Do you know how I do?"

"How?" Carolyn asked curiously.

"Well, when I get downhearted thinking about your leaving, I just try to imagine what it will be like for you in Amarillo, having good times in school. And I tell myself that I ought to be happy because you'll be having a good time."

"Why, Rowena," Carolyn said, deeply moved, "what a nice thing for you to do!"

"Oh, it doesn't always work," Rowena admitted honestly. "Times I can't make myself see anything good at all about it!"

"I'll come home pretty often," Carolyn told her. "I'll come week ends, when the weather's good enough so Dennis and Melinda can bring me. And when I do, I'll try to come over here. You watch, and maybe I'll be here—"

"Rowena!"

A man's voice, terrible in its anger, sounded at their very side. It was Mr. Warren. Both girls jumped guiltily to their feet and stood facing him.

"Rowena," he said sternly, "go to the house, immediately."

Rowena stood there, either too frightened to move or unwilling to do so, even had she been able.

"I said, *go!*"

Rowena turned and started toward the dugout.

"As for you—" The stern man made a gesture in Carolyn's direction. He did not have to finish. His meaning was clear enough. Almost in a single motion, she was at Prince's side, on his back, riding off across the prairie. She did not bother to pick up her little basket in which she had carried her lunch. She did not look back to see Rowena once more. Even had she looked, she could not have seen her friend—because her eyes were filled with tears.

N I N E

CAROLYN SAT UP IN BED, her heart beating very fast. She listened, her ears straining to hear a repetition of whatever it was which had frightened her. She could hear nothing—absolutely nothing—to warrant her fright. In the next bed, Katie was breathing gently; outside, in the chicken house, the hens stirred, then settled down; far off, across the fields in some neighbor's yard, dogs barked. But these were not fearsome noises; they were familiar, comforting sounds which could be heard every night. And yet, something had frightened her enough to waken her from a sound sleep; even now, she was continuing to tremble a little. A bad dream might have done this, but she had not been dreaming.

Perhaps a storm was coming up. No, the night was still and bright.

The night was bright.

The thought sent her scurrying to the window. She stood on a chair, in order to look outside. And when she did, she saw the reason for her fear. A prairie fire was burning, out there in the direction of the Warren place. The light had shone into her bedroom, and that was what had awakened her. Every instinct warned her of the terrible nature of this thing. Prairie fires had been known to spread for a hundred miles or more, taking everything in their path. Winter feed went before them, and houses crisped up like pieces of kindling put into a stove. She ran toward the door, on feet winged with fear, calling as she went, her horror spilling over into her voice.

"Papa, Papa! There's a fire!"

Her words, the way she spoke them, got through to Papa instantly. You had only to say the word "fire" out here, and anyone would jerk awake from the soundest sleep, just as Papa did now.

"Where?" he asked.

"Out there—toward the Warrens'."

His eyes followed her shaking finger as she pointed through the window, although, actually, there was no need to point, for he could see for himself the little red tongues licking up on the horizon. There were only a few now, but they were bright enough to light the night sky—and menacing enough to bring fear to anyone who looked.

Mama was awake, too, standing with Carolyn and Papa, looking out at the dancing little imp-flames.

"Oh!" she cried. "Oh, Robert! Oh—what will you do?"

Already, Papa was dressing.

"I'll ride to get the twins," he planned. "We'll tell the

Cartwrights, if they haven't already seen it. And the Fosters—"

"Thank goodness there's no wind," Mama said.

That was the best thing that could have happened. Wind spread the flames, making it almost impossible to fight them. Mama was right in being grateful for a still night.

"And the Adams boys—" Papa went on, already dressed and starting for the door. "Someone will go for them." He was mentally checking the help that could be mustered against this great need. When fire broke out, you didn't ask people whether they wanted to help fight it. You simply went yourself and took all the neighbors with you.

"I'm off," Papa said, needlessly, for he was well on his way to the corral. In so short a time that you couldn't believe it, he had saddled his horse and was riding in the direction of the fire.

Just at that moment, Katie came into the room, looking very sleepy, her hair hanging down in braids on each side of her head.

"What on earth—" she began.

"A prairie fire," Mama told her.

"A prairie fire!" Katie repeated after her mother, unable to say more. The three of them stood there in the middle of the floor, listening to the sound of Papa's horse, galloping off in the night.

"It's awful," Mama said. "I wish there was something we could do."

Carolyn shivered as she looked through the window again. It seemed to her that the flames were larger and more widely spaced than they had been when she had first looked out, not more than fifteen minutes ago.

"Well," Katie said, wide awake now, "at least there's no wind."

"And there'll be help," Mama reminded the girls. "Papa and the twins and the Cartwrights and the Fosters —oh, all the men will come and help. I just wish there was something we women could do."

"Mama—" Katie said, and her mother turned quickly at the ring of decision in her voice. The family always did, when Katie spoke like that. Perhaps it was because she so seldom made decisions that people jumped to attention when she did. "Mama, there is something. We can make up a lot of sandwiches and some coffee. We can fill the jugs with water. And we can take those things to the men who are fighting the fire."

"Why, of course," Mama said admiringly. "How fine it is of you to think of that, Katie."

And of course it was. The men would probably be fighting the fire the rest of the night, and perhaps even well into tomorrow, before they had it stopped—if they stopped it at all. Carolyn shivered again, thinking of their own house and stock and crops, lying in the path of the destroyer. The men would be hungry and thirsty and tired before they were through, and they would need food and water and coffee to keep them going. Mama was right; Katie's idea was fine.

"And we'll take some lard and some baking soda," Katie went on. "Some of them are sure to get burns, and we can treat them right there."

Across the years, a memory came to Carolyn—Katie burning her hand, trying to make vinegar pie while Mama was back in East Texas, nursing Grandmother. Bryan Cartwright, dropping by and treating the burn with ordinary kitchen soda. She bet Katie was remembering the incident, too. Come to think of it, she hadn't suggested feeding the fire fighters until Mama said the Cartwrights would be helping.

"We'll start getting the things ready right now," Mama said. "Carolyn, you fill all the jugs with water—better get dressed first, for we'll want to be leaving as soon as we can."

Carolyn turned to follow her directions. It was a relief to have some job assigned her. It kept her from thinking too much that she was the only one who had a pretty good idea of how that fire must have started.

Mama was driving the team and Carolyn and Katie sat in the back seat of the spring wagon, with the basket of sandwiches and the jugs of coffee and water at their feet. Carolyn was trying not to think how recently she had ridden along this same path, also carrying food. It wasn't any trouble at all for Mama to find the way, even though there was no moon. The light from the dozens of little, licking flames guided them. Wherever these were, the men to fight them would also be. The main trouble was with the horses. They were so nervous and skittish it was all Mama could do to keep them headed in the right direction. Horses—all animals—were deathly afraid of prairie fires. The Pierce team knew by instinct that the flames meant grave danger for them. Maybe they even sensed that their winter feed, as well as their very lives, was in danger.

"There they are," Katie said quickly.

Sure enough, you could see them, a dozen men or so, silhouetted against the flames. All the neighbors were fighting the fire together.

Mama drove on, keeping a firm hand on the lines because the horses were getting more nervous by the minute.

"I see your father," Mama said. She was able to pick Papa out of the group before Katie or Carolyn could tell one of the moving figures from the other. "Oh, Robert!" she called.

Above the confusion of noise and activity, Papa heard her. He turned and made his way toward the wagon.

"In the name of goodness, Catherine," he said crossly, "what are you doing here? It's not safe—"

Mama ignored that. "We brought some coffee and sandwiches," she told him. "And some water. You men can come back to us in shifts and get something—"

"That's wonderful," Papa said. He hadn't been cross with Mama, really. He had just been scared to see her there, riding right into the face of danger. "They'll be needing it, before this is licked."

"How are things going?" Mama asked.

"We're holding our own," Papa told her. "It isn't gaining on us. It's mighty lucky you saw it, Carolyn! A few hours later and we couldn't have stopped it easily—maybe not at all. Wait—it's catching in a fresh spot!"

Papa was off, on the run, to beat out a new spark which had landed on a dry piece of grass. It was only the smallest bit of a flame, no larger than the end of a burning match, but even that you could not trust. You gave a fire no chance at all—no chance at all.

"I'll send the men back a few at a time," Papa called over his shoulder.

"We'll be ready," Mama said, turning toward the spring wagon. "Katie, get the sandwiches out. Carolyn, have the cups ready."

The men came, two at a time. They ate their sandwiches, drank their coffee, with one eye on the fire. In the gray light of morning, already beginning to coat the sky, they looked tired and drawn. Their faces were streaked with soot and dirt; their shirts, covered with a mixture of dirt and perspiration, stuck to their backs. But they did not seem discouraged.

"How are things going?" Mama asked, as she handed the two Adams boys sandwiches.

"Oh, we'll lick it," they assured her. "Heck, it ain't got a chance, with us after it."

Funny thing, here they were, dirty and grimy and tired, fighting away for the sake of the man they had so lately made the butt of a cruel joke. They were going into this with as much energy and enthusiasm as they ever put into a joke. The Adams boys weren't really bad—just thoughtless, in things that didn't really matter.

Helping a neighbor did matter, and they were throwing themselves into the enterprise with all their might. It was like them to pretend the fire had no chance at all, as long as they were around. But Carolyn noticed that they looked back over their shoulders, even as they spoke. Oh, they knew as well as anyone the dangerous nature of the thing they fought, just as they knew victory was not as easy, or as certain, as they pretended.

"Mighty good sandwiches, Miz Pierce," Hank Adams said, talking with his mouth full. It wasn't just the haste with which he was forced to eat now which made him do this—that was the way the Adams boys did things all the time.

"I guess you didn't let Sprout," Cy Adams jerked his thumb in Carolyn's direction, "mess around with them any. She'd have poisoned us all, for sure." He, too, talked with his mouth full.

Carolyn smiled at them. She knew better than to take those Adams boys seriously.

"Well," Hank said, draining his cup of coffee, "we better get back. Thanks a lot."

The two of them were off together, back to the plow. That was one of the first things you did when a grass fire started—got a plow and a team and started turning furrows between the fire and the grass it was headed toward. Fire couldn't spread in plowed ground.

Almost immediately, two more men came to the spring wagon. Carolyn's heart did a quick little jump. There stood the Fosters, 'Lonzo and Jim.

"Well, hello," Mama said. "So you got home in time for the fire fighting, Jim."

"Yes—rode out for the week end, just in time to get in on the excitement. Hi, Carolyn. Hello, Katie."

"Hello," Carolyn said.

Mama handed each of the Fosters a cup of coffee, and Katie gave them sandwiches. Carolyn noticed that, even though they were in as much a hurry as the Adams boys had been, they didn't gobble, and they didn't talk with their mouths full.

"These are mighty good," Jim said. "It was a smart thing for you to think of, Mrs. Pierce. Helps the fighters a lot."

"It was Katie's idea," Mama told him.

"Good for Katie!" 'Lonzo said.

"Smart girl." Jim smiled his approval.

"How are things going?" Mama asked.

"Oh—we're gaining on it. Our big task now is to keep it from spreading. It's already burned the Warrens' hay—every bit of it—and the pasture. Corral's gone, too, but it was a wreck anyway, so that's no great loss.

The hay—Mr. Warren had been proud of that, Rowena had said. It was something he himself had worked for, something he had salvaged from the hopelessness of this place. And the pasture—feed to last the cow the rest of the summer and fall and well into winter. Oh, it was a terrible thing that had happened to the Warrens! What little success they might have gained was swept away now.

"That's too bad," Mama said sympathetically.

"Could have been a lot worse," Jim told her. "Lucky thing we caught it when we did. The fellow who first saw it sure did the whole community a service."

"It was Carolyn," Mama said. "She woke up and saw it and called her father."

"Oh, she did!" Jim Foster turned to face Carolyn. "Why Carolyn—that was smart of you—"

He wasn't laughing at her now. There was warm approval in his eyes, and in the face of it, Carolyn found herself flushing and looking down at the tips of her shoes as if, maybe, they might give her some clue as to how she should answer him. No words came to her. All she could think of was Jim Foster, sweeping her up behind him on his horse in order to get her across the muddy street. And, also, of his saying, "Who do you think made me want to study in the first place?"

He hadn't been laughing at her that time, either.

145

"You did us all a good turn, Carolyn," he said seriously, draining his cup and handing it back to Mama. "A mighty good turn. Thank you, Mrs. Pierce. You are helping us a great deal."

"It's the least we could do," Mama declared. "I wish there was more."

"Well, now that I think of it, there is," Jim said. "Mrs. Warren and the girl—they're over there in the dugout. We thought it was as safe a place as any for them to stay. They must be scared half to death. You could go over there and—well—sort of comfort them."

"Why, Jim," Mama cried, "what a thoughtful thing for you to suggest! I don't know why it hadn't occurred to me to ask about them earlier. I'll go." She hesitated. "Is—is Mr. Warren there with them?"

Mama was, of course, remembering the other time she had gone to the Warren house and had received no welcome.

"No." Jim Foster grinned. "He's out there, fighting with the rest of us. He's not much good at it, but he's making a big try."

Mr. Warren, Carolyn thought, had joined up with his neighbors. Above the soreness in her heart, the sense of guilt, the regret, that one thought was good to hold onto. Mr. Warren, at long last, was willing to have his neighbors around.

"Katie," Mama decided, "you can serve the rest of the coffee and sandwiches without me. I'm going to Mrs. Warren."

"All right, Mama," Katie said, calm and cool as you please. No shyness now, and no timidity. Her hair had blown every which way in the drive across the prairie,

146

and her sleeves were rolled up above her elbows, but she was as collected as if Mama had told her to do nothing more unusual than to set the table for dinner.

"Carolyn—" Mama began, probably getting ready to suggest that she stay and help Katie.

"Mama," Carolyn broke in, taking no chances, "I want to go with you. Remember—I know Mrs. Warren, and," she hesitated, "and Rowena. I know them all," she finished quickly.

"Of course, Carolyn," Mama agreed. "You should go. I had forgotten you had met the family, that day on the train." She turned to Katie. "You can manage by yourself, can't you?"

"Of course," Katie answered confidently.

Mama and Carolyn walked across the field, the short distance to the dugout. The little window was a square of light, and they moved toward it. Mama, with Carolyn following, walked down the steps and knocked smartly at the door.

"Come—"

Even that single word gave a sense of hopeless fear. Mama opened the door and she and Carolyn walked in.

Mrs. Warren, fully dressed, lay across the bed. Rowena, also dressed, sat on a chair. Both Mrs. Warren and Rowena had a dazed, unreal look on their faces, like animals caught in traps. They didn't seem to know exactly what was going on. Mama's walking in on them was just another part of the whole strange business.

"I'm Mrs. Pierce," Mama said, "Carolyn's mother."

"Yes—" Mrs. Warren replied, scarcely above a whisper.

"Oh, Carolyn!"

Rowena ran across the floor of the little room, to her friend's side. "Oh, Carolyn—we've been so scared! The fire—it just roared and crackled, and we thought it was going to come right here where we were, in the house. Papa was out trying to stop it, and he was getting nowhere at all, and then the men came—"

Carolyn looked closely at Rowena. Fear showed in her face and, now that help had come and her friend was with her, relief. But there was not a trace of guilt. As far as Rowena was concerned, she felt no responsibility for the fire. In a way, Carolyn was a little disappointed. It would have been the most wonderful relief to have confessed her own suspicions in the matter. But she couldn't, now. She couldn't give Rowena any more cause for fear and concern. It seemed to Carolyn, standing there in the middle of the little dugout, that of late her life had been just a series of guilty secrets which, for one reason or another, she couldn't share.

"You're so good—so good to come," Mrs. Warren was telling Mama. "After—"

"I wanted to," Mama broke in, not allowing Mrs. Warren to finish. No need for the woman to say the apology which was on her lips, the apology for the way the Warrens had acted the other time Mama came.

"So good—" Mrs. Warren repeated, evidently touched by Mama's thoughtfulness. "Are they—getting it stopped?"

"They will," Mama assured her confidently. "All the neighbors are out there working."

"Yes, all the neighbors—" Mrs. Warren echoed. Something about the idea of the neighbors fighting to help the Warrens, even after the shabby way they had been treated those other times they had tried to be friendly, was too much for the woman. She began to cry.

"They are all so—so kind," she sobbed. "I—I didn't think I could stand it, waiting, not knowing. But they said I would be safer here, and I've waited—"

"You poor, dear thing!" Mama exclaimed. "Listen—you're coming home with me. Do you understand? Right now. I'm taking you until things get worked out—here—" She made a gesture in the direction of the dugout, then the burning grass. And, just as her children always took Mama's decisions at times of crisis, so did Mrs. Warren accept her idea now. She made no protest at all. Instead, she turned toward Mama, apparently feeling only a great gladness to do what she said.

Mama walked across to Mrs. Warren. She put her arm around the woman's thin shoulders and drew her close.

"Now, now," she said, "everything is going to be all right. Stop crying—"

Over her shoulder, Mama said to Carolyn, "You go tell Katie to set out the last of the coffee and food. And then to drive here, to the house. Tell her we are going to take Mrs. Warren and Rowena home with us, and come back with more coffee and food."

"All right," Carolyn replied, turning to carry out Mama's orders.

"Rowena," Mama went on, "you start collecting some things you and your mother will need. I'm going to keep you for several days."

Carolyn walked toward the spring wagon where Katie was still serving the coffee and sandwiches. Two men were walking away—actually, a man and a boy. That would probably be Mr. Warren and his son, Van. Van was only a boy, but he was out fighting with the rest of them, a fact which probably made all the men think the more of him. For some reason she could not quite place, Carolyn felt a surge of pride in his actions; almost, she thought, as if it had been one of the twins who had been proving himself. Somehow, the Warrens belonged to her by now. Even as she was thinking this, she saw another figure coming toward Katie and the wagon. It was Bryan Cartwright. Carolyn halted in her swift approach. This was something for Katie to handle—and alone.

"Hello." Bryan spoke a little gruffly. "They told me there was some coffee here—"

"Yes," Katie said quietly, "there is. I'll pour you a cup. Help yourself to a sandwich."

She filled a tin cup with coffee. She put in two teaspoonfuls of sugar and tilted the tin of milk to let just the least little bit drip into the cup.

"That right?" she asked, handing it to him.

"Yes," he answered softly, "you remembered—"

He meant she remembered he liked two teaspoonfuls of sugar and, as they used to tease him, not enough milk to make it worth-while to put it in.

"Yes," she said, "why shouldn't I?"

And then, anxiously, as he reached awkwardly with his left hand to take the cup from her, she cried, "What's the matter—have you been hurt?"

"Nothing—" he said, apparently either unwilling to have her know or ashamed that he should have been careless enough to get himself injured. "It's nothing."

Katie was out of the wagon and down beside him in a flash. "Let me see," she ordered, sounding just like Mama when one of the children had been hurt. And, when he held his right hand stubbornly behind him, she repeated firmly, *"Let me see."*

She didn't sound one bit frightened or uncertain of herself, the way she had around him during the last few months. She just seemed determined and sure. She was so concerned about him that she forgot altogether about being scared on her own account. Suddenly, although she couldn't have told why, something came back to Carolyn. Katie, killing the snake the time she thought it was going to hurt her little sister—the same Katie who was so scared of snakes herself she got pale if anyone even said the word. But there she had been, pounding the very life out of that snake, never giving herself a thought. When she got through, it was, as the twins had said, the deadest snake in all the Panhandle of Texas! Now, as she was insisting on seeing Bryan's hand, she had that same look of being lifted out of herself and her own fears.

Bryan, recognizing the authority in her voice, slowly extended his right hand. Even from where Carolyn stood, she could see the burn on it, spreading over most of the back of his hand and running up on his wrist.

"It's nothing," he told Katie again.

She didn't even answer him. Instead, she turned back to the wagon and got out the white rags, the soda and the lard she had brought for just such an emergency. She tore a wide strip of soft cloth. She scooped up a generous bit of lard and spread it over the surface of the burn. Then she put on soda, her face intent and earnest as she worked. Carolyn stole a look at Bryan as he stood there, quietly submitting to her sister's aid. If six or seven angels had been beside him, his face couldn't have been more bright

151

and shining. Katie tied a string around the bandage, making it secure.

"There," she said, dropping his hand. "Feel better?"

"Yes," he answered, speaking softly. "Yes." He seemed lost in thought. "Do you remember one time when *you* got burned, and I bandaged your hand?" he asked.

"Yes—" Katie was speaking softly, too, now, also lost in memory. "Yes—"

"You were making pies," he said. "A whole kitchen full of pies. And you knew as much about pie making as I did about—well—" he hesitated, came up with what, for him, seemed to be the most convincing words, "as I know about music and painting."

"I learned," Katie told him steadily. "I can make a good pie now. I learned, just as you could about—music and painting—and such things."

"I wonder—" Bryan was beginning, when someone hurried toward the wagon, calling as he came.

"Come along, Bryan! We think it's breaking out in a new place."

Bryan was never to finish his sentence. He was off at a run, forgetting even to say good-by or thank you. Katie stood perfectly still, looking after him, so lost in thought that Carolyn could scarcely bring herself to interrupt. It was several minutes before she got herself together enough to walk toward her sister, in order to deliver her mother's message. Finally, however, she did.

"Katie—" she said. "Katie—"

Katie seemed to come back from a long distance. She shook herself.

"Yes," she answered.

"Mama says—" Carolyn began—and then went on to give Mama's message, word for word.

"I'll be there right away," Katie told her. "Help me set the things out, Carolyn."

T E N

THE HOUSE WAS VERY full of people. Everywhere Carolyn went, the place was spilling over. At night, there
was Rowena, sleeping on a cot in the room Carolyn shared
with Katie; by day, there was Rowena at her side.

"Oh, Carolyn, I can't tell you how wonderful it is to
be with people—to be with *you!*"

Rowena looked so neat, so pretty, so happy at the turn
things had taken that Carolyn couldn't do anything but
rejoice with her.

"I know it is selfish and wrong of me, but I'm glad the
fire happened," she went on. "Even if it did burn up our
hay and the corral and the rest of it. I'm still glad."

She looked at Carolyn eagerly, hoping, apparently, to
find understanding, not condemnation, of her confession.

"Do you blame me?" she asked. "I mean, do you think
I'm selfish and—well—wicked?"

"I should say not," Carolyn assured her. "I don't blame you a bit."

Actually, she didn't. It was herself she blamed, and she needed more than anything in the world to have a talk with Mama about things. Only, there was no getting her mother off by herself. Just now, she was in the sitting room with Mrs. Warren, who was sewing buttons on the dresses Mama had made for Carolyn to have for school this fall. Mrs. Warren had insisted until Mama had found some work for her to do.

"I would feel better," she declared, "if I could help. I am really good with a needle. Please give me something to do."

So Mama found some mending, and Mrs. Warren finished it so quickly and so well that everyone was amazed.

"I should say you are good," Mama said. "You work so skillfully and so nicely—it's amazing."

"Give me more," Mrs. Warren begged.

Mama brought out the more difficult things, like buttonholes and hems to take up. Mrs. Warren went through these with equal ease and skill. She worked quickly and smoothly. In the three days since the fire, she seemed to have improved visibly in health and spirits. Her cheeks were beginning to have a little pink in them; her eyes were bright and happier. Perhaps, like Rowena, she was glad the fire had happened.

"You are so good to us," she told Mama, stitching away as if her very life depended on getting the work exactly right. "I hadn't believed there was such kindness in the whole world—"

"Nonsense," Mama protested. "It's good to have you.

Company is an occasion out here. We look forward to it and dread having it leave."

"I can't get over it," Mrs. Warren marveled, shaking her head in a puzzled gesture. "You make it sound as if *we* were doing you a favor by being here. "

"Well, aren't you?" Mama laughed. "And now I'd better go start supper!"

You couldn't stop Mama and talk to her while she was cooking a meal, even if the kitchen hadn't been full of people, too. Papa and Mr. Warren were there, with pencils and bits of paper, figuring things out. The kitchen table was covered with sheets of paper, all filled with numbers. Papa was looking serious and business-like. Mr. Warren was interested and alert. He wasn't cross now, or angry, or upset. He looked years younger and much, much nicer.

"The trouble was all with me," he was saying. "I wasn't meant to farm, and I jumped into it without knowing the first thing about it. I should never have come out here, to begin with, but I have been too proud—or should I say conceited—to admit this. It took a fire and a lot of wonderful neighbors pitching in to help me, in spite of the way I had acted, to jolt ordinary common sense and good manners back in me. I'll regret the way I acted all my life."

"Now see here, Warren," Papa told him firmly, "this country isn't made up entirely of farmers. It takes all kinds to keep a country going. If you want to farm, it's good land—the best. But if you don't, it's also a good land in which to work at your particular trade. We'd be in a fine mess out here if everybody tried farming—just as we'd be in a fine mess everywhere with just farmers and nobody else."

"Yes," Mr. Warren agreed, "I can see that. Where I made my mistake was blaming the country for what I, myself, was unable to do."

Papa let that pass. "The way I see it," he said, "you are, primarily, a storekeeper."

"Yes," Mr. Warren said, "I had a store of my own for many years—"

"In that case, there is a job open to you," Papa went on. "A neighbor of ours—young Jim Foster—has been helping in a store in Amarillo. He is leaving for school in a few weeks. The owner has been looking for someone to take his place, preferably a man with some experience in book work, as well as in selling. Jim told him about you, and he'd like to have you come in and talk with him."

You would have thought Papa had given Mr. Warren the greatest gift in the world by the way his face lighted up. He looked happy and full of courage and purpose.

"I—" he began. "I don't know how to thank you. But," he went on, doubt coming to him, "there is the— well, the claim. I can't just walk off and leave it. I mean, I could, but I shouldn't."

Carolyn liked him for saying that. He had taken out the claim and it was his responsibility. He really couldn't just walk off and leave it.

"There is an offer for it, too," Papa said. "A young neighbor of ours, you know him—Bryan Cartwright—has been anxious to rent some extra land. He says, in case you want to take the job in town, he'd like to have first chance at renting your place."

Mr. Warren laid down the pencil with which he had been figuring. He seemed to have some trouble in getting started on what he wanted to say. He cleared his throat and finally managed to speak. "I can't get over it! All this kindness from people I had been—well, even rude to." He hesitated, then turned to Carolyn, who was standing there, uncertain whether to start helping Mama or to go to the chicken house and help Van, who was gathering eggs. You never saw people so anxious to work as these Warrens!

"Carolyn," Mr. Warren said, "I need to do a lot of apologizing, and I might as well start with you. I am embarrassed and ashamed of the way I acted toward you. You have done so much for us—shared your lunch that day on the train, helped Rowena, and then, finally, spotted the fire which might even have cost us our lives, but for you—"

He stopped, apparently unable to go on.

"Oh, that's all right," Carolyn mumbled.

Then she turned and left the room. One thing she knew for sure. She was going to talk to Mama. Crowds of people or not, she was going to find a time *soon* when she could get her mother off by herself and unburden her soul of all the things lying so heavily upon it.

Carolyn found her chance after supper was over, and the dishes were all washed and back in place. She did not, however, get it without some effort on her part.

"Mama," she said urgently, "I have to see you."

Mama, setting sponge to rise for tomorrow's bread, looked at her uncertainly.

"Is it very important, Carolyn? I thought Mrs. Warren and I would start putting the lace on your slips this evening. She seems to feel better about being here if I let her keep busy."

"It is very important, Mama," Carolyn told her with

determination. "I will wait until you start Mrs. Warren on the lace, but I must see you."

Mama looked at her keenly. "Why, you poor darling," she finally said, "I've neglected you entirely, with all those others underfoot. Of *course* I can see you."

As soon as the sponge was set aside with a white cloth covering it, Mama and Carolyn found themselves in Mama's room, without anybody else around to interrupt.

"Now," Mama demanded, "what is it, honey?"

"Oh, Mama!" Carolyn wailed. "Oh, Mama!"

"Tell me," Mama urged. "Tell me everything—"

Carolyn did not need the command; she needed only the opportunity. It all spilled out from the beginning— how she had first seen Rowena, purely by accident, and how the other meetings grew out of that.

"There wasn't anything wrong in seeing Rowena," Mama remarked quietly.

"Oh, no—but I didn't do it in the right way at all. I started keeping things from you, and then it went on, and I got deeper and deeper into it."

"I see," Mama said.

"I honestly thought I ought to go see Rowena. She was so—well, so lonesome and all—"

"And so you should," Mama agreed. "But why you felt you had to keep it a secret is beyond me."

"I really can't understand that, either," Carolyn confessed. "I mean, I can't see why I wanted to keep it from you. Except, of course, I *had* promised Meg I wouldn't tell."

"Yes," Mama mused, "you had given your word."

"We were both foolish," Carolyn went on. "I can see it now. But anyway, we couldn't let Mr. Warren know."

"Yes," Mama admitted, "I can see how it was difficult."

She was silent, thinking things over. Finally she spoke. "That's one of the hard things about growing up, Carolyn," she said. "It's difficult to draw a clear-cut line between what is right and what is wrong. Rowena certainly needed companionship. But if her father had forbidden it—oh, dear, I don't know what I, myself, would have done in that case!"

Carolyn looked at her mother in amazement. "You mean—" she began uncertainly.

Mama sensed her confusion.

"Yes," she said, "I mean grown people are often uncertain about what is right for them to do. They have to think about it and work at it, and sometimes even then they get mixed up. Life is not easy, Carolyn. You must know that by now. Even when we try hard, it is not easy. We must do the best we know how, and hope things will work out."

Carolyn considered her mother's words soberly. Growing up wasn't as wonderful as she had thought it was going to be. She could see all sorts of unpleasant things stretching out ahead of her—responsibilities and uncertainties and disappointments. For one swift, wild moment she wanted to cry out to Mama that she didn't want to grow up at all, ever. It meant only trouble and difficulties.

"But," Mama went on, "life is still a very wonderful thing, Carolyn. All those difficulties and troubles—they are balanced by rewards and pleasures. You will see—you will understand when they come to you."

I'm having one of the rewards right now, Carolyn thought. Sitting here talking with Mama, as if I'm already grown and able to figure things out for myself. Somehow, she felt she ought to pay for this privilege.

"I'm sorry, Mama," she said humbly. "I'm sorry I deceived you. It started out so—well, so easy and not my doing at all. And then, suddenly, I was in it and it seemed to grow, all of its own self. Before long, it had become too big for me."

"That's the way with deceptions," Mama told her. "They do get out of hand. They're like a grass fire—start little, end up big."

"Oh, Mama!" Carolyn cried. "That's it—that's the whole trouble! Everyone's praising me for seeing the fire—"

"Well, you did see it first," Mama pointed out sensibly. "You saw it and called your father—"

"I saw it because—because—well, Mama—" Even then the confession did not come easily.

"Yes," Mama said. "Go on, Carolyn. You saw it because—?" She did not finish, either.

"I saw it because I think I'm the one who started it," Carolyn told her. It was a relief to have the words out at last.

"You started it?" Mama echoed. She wasn't a bit calm now. "What a silly thing to say!" And then she went on more evenly, "All right—tell me everything."

Carolyn did what she had wanted to do for so long. She gave all the details about the picnic, from the building of the little fire, right on down to her leaving so hastily because Mr. Warren had come upon the two of them, picnicking there in the bed of the creek. Mama listened, not interrupting in any way.

161

"So you see, Mama," Carolyn finished, "why I feel so guilty when people praise me for seeing the fire."

"Yes," Mama agreed thoughtfully. "Yes, I see—"

"What must I do, Mama?" Carolyn asked. "Should I tell everyone? I mean, shouldn't I tell people Rowena and I built the fire?"

"Let me think—" Mama said.

She thought a long time. Finally she spoke.

"Have you mentioned your—well, your idea—to Rowena?" she asked.

"No, Mama."

Carolyn wanted to explain that she couldn't bear to say anything to her friend which might interrupt the happiness she seemed to feel, here at the Pierce place, with things beginning to work out for her family.

"Do you think she, also, feels your fire might have been responsible?"

"No," Carolyn answered, "I've watched her, and I've even talked to her a little bit, trying to feel her out. She doesn't seem to have any idea at all that we—that we—"

Carolyn couldn't finish.

"Well," Mama asked briskly, "do you honestly know for sure you *did?* I mean, did you see a spark fly away or anything else happen which might have caused a fire?"

"Why, no," Carolyn told her, "I didn't. We were awfully careful. Rowena built the fire down in the creek bed, and it was just a little one, there on bare ground. We let it die down to ashes before we put the eggs in to roast."

Mama frowned thoughtfully.

"Of course," she decided finally, "we'll have to talk to your father about this. But for the time being, I think you had better not mention the matter to Rowena—or to anyone else—for Rowena's sake. She has had a hard time. No need to add to her troubles now, unless we could be sure."

"Of course, Mama," Carolyn agreed. She had needed to ease her own sense of guilt by confessing. Now she could see that, to do so, she must also implicate Rowena, who had actually built the fire. This would be putting a burden of guilt on someone who had already suffered a great deal.

"Sometimes," Mama pointed out wisely, "it's harder to keep still than it is to speak. As I have said, we must talk to Papa about this, but at the moment, it seems the kindest thing would be—since you aren't sure it was your campfire which started it all—to keep quiet and not make things any harder for Rowena."

"Yes, Mama," Carolyn said.

She could see Mama's point. Telling when she wasn't sure might relieve her conscience, but couldn't help anything. In fact, it might even hurt Rowena. Another adult responsibility, awesome and fearful, loomed up before her. Grown people had to learn the difference between the time to talk and the time to keep silent.

"Well," Mama decided, "I'll speak to Papa about this, Carolyn. And," she paused, looking at her daughter thoughtfully, "I don't know when a thing has pleased me more than your feeling free to talk with me. Now I must see your father."

She stood up and started to leave the room. As she did so, she looked out the window at a man who had just ridden up on horseback.

"Why I do believe that's Bryan Cartwright," she said.

"Your father said he would probably come over to talk with Mr. Warren about renting the place."

She left hastily. Carolyn went to her own room. Right now, she wanted very much to be alone.

She was not to have her wish, however, for when she reached the room, there was Katie. She was looking excited and white around the mouth and very upset.

"What's wrong, Katie?" Carolyn asked. And then, almost immediately, she caught herself. She *knew* what was wrong.

"He's out there," Katie said, speaking in a strange sort of voice. "I saw him—he has just come. Do you suppose," she asked anxiously, "oh, Carolyn, do you think he has come to call on me?"

Carolyn shifted uncomfortably. It hurt her to see Katie looking like that, so excited and hopeful, thinking Bryan had come to see her. She couldn't make herself look at her sister, for if she did, Katie would guess she knew the reason for his coming—that it was just to talk about renting land from Mr. Warren.

"You know," Katie said accusingly, "you know why he's here. And it's not to see me. Tell me."

Carolyn hesitated.

"Tell me." Katie insisted.

"It's to see Mr. Warren—about renting his land," Carolyn confessed almost in a whisper.

"Oh!" Katie said. Her chin began to tremble, like that of a child who had been hurt unjustly. "Oh, Carolyn—whatever makes him act the way he does?"

Carolyn was silent.

"If I could just talk to him," Katie went on. "If I could just get him off to myself and talk to him."

"It wouldn't do a bit of good," Carolyn told her, stung by the hurt in Katie's face. That Bryan Cartwright—he was a fine one to be hurting Katie like this! He wasn't worth one worry she was wasting on him. "It wouldn't do a bit of good," Carolyn repeated firmly. After all, she knew a thing or two about Bryan Cartwright.

Katie looked at her quickly.

"How do you know?" she asked.

"Because I talked to him myself," Carolyn confessed. "And he was just horrid. He wouldn't listen to me, and he laughed at me, and he was rude—"

"You talked to him?" Katie came alive, as if someone had stuck her with a pin. She came over to Carolyn, put her hands on her sister's shoulders.

"Now you tell me," she demanded. "You tell me everything."

Carolyn didn't hesitate a minute. She started right in telling Katie all about it—how she had schemed to find an opportunity to talk to Bryan and how, at last, she had found it; how she had come right out and told him he wasn't treating Katie right and that she, Katie, felt perfectly awful about it; how Bryan had said that she, Katie, wasn't meant for a farm, and how she oughtn't to be on one at all.

"Oh, he did, did he?" Katie interrupted. Her face was beginning to brighten, like a sky after a storm has passed. "He said that, did he?"

"He certainly did," Carolyn assured her. "And I told him you could do things like anybody else—cook and keep house and the rest of it. And that you were brave, when you needed to be—"

"Brave, am I?" Katie mused. "Oh, Carolyn—I'm the biggest coward! And," she added quickly, "the biggest idiot."

"You are not," Carolyn told her hotly. "And I'm sorry I—well, that I meddled in your affairs."

"Somebody needed to," Katie assured her briskly. "Now suppose you tell me the rest of it."

Carolyn went on to finish the story, not skipping any details, even to how Bryan told her to get along and stop meddling in grown-ups' affairs.

"Well," Katie exclaimed, "so he said that, too, did he?"

She stopped, got up and moved restlessly around the room. Finally she came back to where Carolyn sat, silent and ashamed.

"Now, little sister," she said, "you scoot. I've got some thinking to do."

She looks just like she did the time she told me she was going to the coal house for coal, when we were caught in the blizzard at the schoolhouse—determined and sure and sort of scared, too, Carolyn thought. That time, I went with her to help. This time, I can't do a thing. I've ruined everything for her, and I can't do a thing to help. She stood up.

"I'm sorry, Katie," she apologized miserably. "I wanted to help—honest, I did."

Katie hugged her sister close. "You helped—better than you know," she said. "You helped. Now scoot."

Carolyn scooted.

There was one place she knew she could be alone, and she went there now. It was the only place, with the whole

house and yard teeming with people! Looking around to
be sure no one saw her, she separated—very carefully, so
as not to injure them—the morning-glory vines which
trailed up the windmill tower. She squeezed through the
opening she had made. Once inside, she found herself in
a green and lovely tent.

She sat down on the grass, feeling a great sense of relief. Outside, she could hear familiar and comforting
sounds—voices in earnest conversation; doors opening and
closing. She could see the house, even the room where
Katie sat "thinking." Dusk was beginning to fall, so Mama
had lighted a lamp in the living room, but in Katie's
room, there was no light.

Katie had not said, "Stay with me, Carolyn, and let me
talk to you," any more than Mama had said, "We'll go
talk to Papa." They had both shut Carolyn out. Perhaps
they thought, as she herself did, that she had made such
a mess of things, no one should dare consult with her on
any important problem.

She shifted her gaze away from the house, in the direction of the corral where Papa, Mr. Warren and Bryan
were talking earnestly. She thought again how good-looking Bryan was, and then she hardened her heart against
him, remembering his treatment of Katie and his abrupt-
ness to herself.

"Well," she heard Bryan say now, "I'm glad you feel
that way."

"It's a fine opportunity," Mr. Warren replied.

The two men shook hands.

"I'll be coming back in the next day or two," Bryan told
him, "and we'll sign the necessary papers."

"Your word is good enough," Mr. Warren assured him.

"I'll let things go the way we've talked it over. Mr. Pierce, here, can be witness to what we have said."

Carolyn couldn't believe what she heard. Mr. Warren, taking the word of a man who lived here in this region; the word of people who, so recently, he had forbidden to come on his place. She knew he had had a change of heart, but this showed how complete it was.

"Well," Bryan agreed, "if that's the way you want it to be, it suits me fine. Guess I'd better be moving along now."

"Good night."

"Good night."

Papa and Mr. Warren turned and walked toward the house. Bryan stood there, his hand linked lightly through his bridle rein, apparently in no hurry to leave, for all he had just announced his intention to do so. As a matter of fact, he seemed to be trying to find an excuse to stay. He made his way over to the windmill tank, leading his horse. Once there, he removed the bridle so as to give the animal a chance to drink. It no more than touched its nose to the water; it wasn't thirsty at all. But Bryan still lingered, looking toward the house several times. And then his face changed, so quickly that Carolyn herself looked in the direction of the house, to find out what had startled him.

There came Katie, walking down the grassy path which led from the house to the windmill, her shoulders set in an attitude of great purpose, her head held high. She wore the air which was always hers when she was undertaking a difficult thing. Bryan took one quick look and then turned his head, apparently meaning to ignore her entirely, once she reached him. Carolyn could have told

him he was making a mistake. When Katie had that determined look on her, there was no ignoring her or brush-
ing her off lightly. Bryan might as well prepare to listen
to her, for that was what he was going to do, in spite of
himself.

"Bryan," Katie began, even before she had reached him.

He turned to face her; no pretense now of not knowing
she was there. But his head was thrown back and he was
braced against her, even before she started. Carolyn's
heart ached for her sister and the difficulty she was about
to encounter.

"Bryan," Katie said again, stopping directly in front of
him, "I want to talk to you."

"You want to talk to me?" Bryan repeated, his words
cool enough, but his manner of saying them not cool at
all. He sounded as if he were holding himself in by a
great effort—as if, maybe, had he followed his own wishes,
he would have run to meet her and grabbed her up in his
arms. Carolyn realized, to her dismay, that she was eaves-
dropping on something which was none of her business at
all. She would have left, fast enough, but that wasn't
possible now. She would just have to stay as quiet as possible and wait until they had finished their talk and gone
away.

"Yes," Katie said softly, "I want to know why—why you
have acted so strangely these last months."

Bryan was silent, not looking at her.

Oh, you'd better answer her, Bryan, Carolyn wanted to
call to him. She's bound to get to the bottom of the
matter. You can't hush her up, the way you did me.
That's our Katie. When she decides a thing needs to be

done, she'll do it and there's no stopping her. Thinking this, Carolyn wasn't sorry for Katie any more.

"Why?" Katie insisted stubbornly.

"I—I don't understand you," Bryan faltered, looking down at the toes of his boots, the way the twins used to do when Mama had caught them, red-handed, in mischief.

"Oh, yes you do," Katie told him. "You've been rude and hateful and—just—just awful, ever since I got back from school. You have! And I can't stand it—I just can't—"

The very thought of his actions seemed too much for her to bear; she began to cry. The great tears simply poured out of her eyes and slid down her cheeks. Bryan couldn't stand it either. He was at her side, his hand on her shoulder.

"Don't cry, Katie," he begged. "Please don't cry."

Katie made no effort to stop. Those tears had been bottled up in her for a long time. She probably couldn't have stopped them had she wanted to.

"You h-hate me," she sobbed. "All the t-time you act as if you h-hate me."

Bryan's hand on her shoulder tightened. He gave her a little shake, half-angry, half-tender.

"*I—hate—you,*" he said, punctuating every word with a shake. "I hate you! How silly can a girl get?"

"Well, you act as if you do," Katie gulped, stopping her tears a little and looking up at him.

Bryan dropped his arms.

"Now listen here, Katie Pierce," he told her roughly, "you know better than that."

"And how should I know better—and why?" Katie's cheeks were very red now, and Carolyn knew it was anger which made them so. "Just tell me how I'd know. Every time you see me, you act as if I'm a poison loco weed, or something."

Bryan didn't answer.

"Is it because you don't want me to—to paint—and play —and sing?" she asked.

Oh, Carolyn thought, so she caught on! So she's taken what I told her and worked it into a reason for talking to Bryan.

He looked at Katie, startled, seeming to wonder how she had ever figured that one out. "You know better than that," he told her shortly.

"I've done those things all my life, since I was a little thing. No use to start holding them against me now."

"Because," Bryan said, "because girls who can do things like that—as well as you can do them—don't belong out here."

"And may I ask you why—if they *want* to be here?" Katie asked him coolly.

"Because—they ought to be someplace where—where they can have more advantages," Bryan faltered.

"I don't know of any greater advantages for a girl," Katie went on steadily, "than to be where she wants to be, with the people she loves most." She turned to face him. "Oh, Bryan," she cried, "what makes you so blind, so stupid? Do I have to say—*everything?*"

Bryan didn't answer.

Then Katie—Katie the timid one, the one afraid of her own shadow, the one who always stood back and let others take the lead—did a very strange thing. She stood on tiptoe and lightly, very lightly, kissed Bryan Cartwright.

"Foolish Bryan!" she said and turned and started to

walk off toward the house—although, Carolyn noticed above her own surprise, there wasn't much purpose in her sister's movements.

She didn't take more than one step—maybe not even a full one at that—before Bryan reached out and pulled her to him.

"Katie," he kept saying, over and over, "Katie—darling!"

Then he was kissing her. My goodness, was he ever kissing her! He acted as if he never meant to stop. Katie wasn't trying to prevent him, either. Much as Carolyn wanted to watch, she resolutely turned her back. All she could hope for was that he'd quit before too long. She certainly didn't want to spend half the night crouched down here in the morning-glory vines.

ELEVEN

CAROLYN WALKED DOWN the street in Amarillo, trying to take in everything she saw. This was her town now, she told herself. Yesterday, Dennis and Melinda had brought her back with them, saying she might as well come a few days before school started, just in order to get herself settled. Mama hadn't objected to Carolyn's leaving several days ahead of time. She thought it was a good idea. She probably realized that, by doing things this way, there wouldn't be any time for Carolyn to feel the strange little ache at parting. So, almost before she knew it, Carolyn found herself, together with her clothes and books and belongings, established in Melinda's guest room, which was to be her home for much of the next four years.

Come to think of it, though, Mama hadn't really had

much time to think about her youngest daughter, anyway. After Katie had worked things out with Bryan, she rushed into the house to say that they were going to be married right away. Well, anyway, some time before Christmas, and nobody—*nobody*—was going to stop them. Of course, nobody was going to try, for it was the thing everyone had been wanting for weeks.

All Mama could do was to put her arms around Katie and croon, "Oh, darling!" Then she cried a little and kissed her daughter. Katie certainly came in for a lot of kissing that evening!

In the excitement of Katie's announcement, everyone was too busy to think much about the fact that Carolyn was leaving home a few days earlier than had been expected.

Carolyn looked around her now as she walked along with a letter to mail for Melinda. "I'm late getting it off, Carolyn," her sister had said. "Will you take it to the station and hand it to the mail clerk when the train comes in?"

The errand suited Carolyn exactly. It gave her much pleasure to realize that she knew several people she met on the way, and they knew her, calling her by name when they spoke. All the people in this town—probably seven thousand by now, Dennis said—were, in a way, her people, too. All the fine things in the town—the electric lights and telephones and water works; the Opera House, where thrilling programs would come this winter—all these were hers, as were the stores and, most especially, the red brick schoolhouse where she would spend much of her time during her stay here.

Three blocks down and several blocks to the left was

Elizabeth's house. Already, the two friends had planned that, when Monday and registration time came, they would walk together to the high school and there, again together, sign up as Freshmen. Was ever a girl as fortunate as she, Carolyn Pierce, found herself to be? She smiled a little, remembering the childish fears she had known earlier in the summer, thinking she would never make friends here, never get used to the school and its ways.

Four blocks in the opposite direction and a little to the left was another house with meaning to Carolyn. It was a small house, but it was running over with happiness. And, even though the family had been in it only a week, it was neat and clean and in order. The Warrens lived here, now that Mr. Warren had a job in the store where Jim Foster had worked. Already, Melinda and Carolyn had gone to call on the family.

"I'll go to school," Rowena exulted as the two girls went out to talk things over while Mrs. Warren and Melinda discussed grown-up matters. "I'll see other girls every day. Not you, Carolyn, because I won't be in high school until next year. But I'll have friends—" The prospect was so wonderful she paused to regard it silently.

"We'll see each other plenty," Carolyn told her. "After school, and other times."

"As soon as Mama feels better," Rowena went on, "she's going to advertise that she'll do mending. *Fine* mending," she added proudly.

"That will be wonderful," Carolyn said.

"And she will have classes to teach young ladies how to do fancy work. My mama knows how to do that better than anyone." There was, apparently, no limit to the pride Rowena could feel in her family and their achievements. . . . "Know what?" she asked after a pause. And then, as if she couldn't wait for Carolyn's answer, she continued, "my papa says he thinks this is a fine country—just the best. He's sorry he—well, he acted the way he did when we first came down."

"He had a lot of bad things happen to him," Carolyn reminded her friend. "No wonder he couldn't see much good here, at first."

"Yes, I know," Rowena mused, her face momentarily saddened at the thought of those past troubles. "But you would have thought the fire was the worst thing that could have happened to us; yet see all the good which came of it. I just don't understand," she finished thoughtfully. "Those other hard things, they just made him stay away from everyone, but the big, hard thing—the fire—made him learn to like people."

"I guess it was because he let people help him this last time," Carolyn decided. "Papa says that's what people are for, out here. To help each other."

"Yes," Rowena agreed. "Yes—I guess that's it."

Personally, Carolyn wanted to get the subject away from that fire as soon as she could. Papa had finally decided Mr. Warren must be told of her feeling of guilt about the destructive blaze. The latter had replied that he felt quite sure the girls' campfire had not been responsible. He himself had been careful to put it out, before he left the spot. Of course, a spark might have escaped earlier, but he did not think it likely. Still, one could not dismiss the possibility entirely. However, he hoped Carolyn would not feel it necessary to tell anyone.

So Carolyn found herself holding fast to the doubt

and uncertainty which, she supposed, would never really leave her. Always there would be the wonder, the half-fear. And always there would be the feeling that she did not have the right to unburden herself of her secret.

"Anyway," Rowena went on, "I'm not going to think about those old, hard times. I'm just going to think about going to school and all that sort of thing—"

Yes, Carolyn thought now, as she walked along remembering Rowena's words, she guessed it had been right to do things the way Mr. Warren wanted.

When she arrived at the station, no train was yet in sight, but it must be close to time, for a few people were standing around, waiting to meet someone, or preparing to leave themselves. Then she saw Jim Foster, with his bag on the platform beside him. Carolyn's heart did a little beat and a skip, thinking what that suitcase meant. Even as she watched, he picked it up and walked over to where she stood.

"Hello," he said.

"Hello."

"I haven't seen you since the night of the fire," he told her.

The fire again! She supposed it would be a long time before she stopped hearing about it.

"You leaving for school?" she asked.

"Yes—"

It was the strangest thing, but when he said that, he looked a little scared—the way she knew she had at the beginning of the summer, when all there was to look forward to was a strange school in a strange town. For Jim, Austin would be different and alien, with newness all around and no knowledge of how to cope with it. Re-

membering, a warm, impulsive kindness came over Carolyn and a great wish to help him, because, in a different
way and in a different town, he would be facing a similar
situation.

"You'll get along fine, Jim," she assured him. "You'll
learn quickly, and you'll make friends. At first, it will all
seem new and strange, but you'll catch on—fast."

He looked at her earnestly. Maybe she just imagined
it, but this time there seemed to be something like relief
in his face.

"You'll learn fast and get good grades, and, by-and-by,
you'll be a lawyer and we'll all be proud of you," she
went on encouragingly.

"Oh, you will, will you?" he asked gruffly.

"Yes, we will," she told him. And then, laughing and
drawing upon her old childhood tricks, she said, "We'll
be *'scruciatingly* proud of you."

He didn't laugh, the way she thought he would. My
goodness, did he think she didn't know any better?

"Carolyn," he began, speaking in a strange sort of
voice, "when you people got to Amarillo, your father
couldn't meet you because he had ridden to get the doctor
for me. I was sick, very sick. He saved my life."

"Yes," Carolyn told him, "I remember. We waited for
him, and I wandered off and got lost."

"Yes, I'm coming to that. The first time I saw you, I
thought—oh, what if anything had happened to her because her father had been away getting help for me? I
thought and I thought about it. Now don't ask me why,
but, some way, that incident always made me feel closer
to you."

"I thought it was because I used big words," Carolyn

reminded him, smiling a little, not quite knowing how to meet this new turn in the conversation.

He grinned slowly. "That was it, too," he said. "But that came later—"

Far down the tracks, she heard the train whistle. Distant it was—and lonesome sounding and even a little sad. The train came on, relentlessly, like time passing. Nobody was going to stop it. Pretty soon, it would pull into the station, pause briefly and then be off again. This time it would have a special passenger. Jim Foster would be on it. And when it left, nothing would ever be the same for him again.

Jim must have been thinking much the same thing, for he turned to her now, quickly and impulsively. "I'll be gone in just a few minutes," he told her.

"Yes—"

"I'll be gone for four years. Four years, I'll be away from here, except for a few vacations, and I'll have to work then to make money to go on."

"Yes—"

Four years! That was an eternity—time-without-end.

"When I am through school—and I'm going to finish and make you all proud of me, just the way you said—when I am through, I'll be twenty-two years old."

Twenty-two years old! A man's age, responsible and adult.

"And when I've finished, I'll come back here," he told her. "I used to think I'd go somewhere else, some big city, far away from here. But now I know I won't. I'll come back here, to this town."

He would come back. The day seemed, suddenly, more wonderful—the sky bluer, the sunshine brighter.

179

"It's like the piece of Scripture you read at the missionary program," he said. "This is a good land—it's a good place to be. Ever since that day, I've been thinking. You helped me, Carolyn, by reading that. It was as if you were talking directly to me, because at the time, I still wasn't sure what I wanted to do."

She had helped him! She wished she could find words to tell him how much he had helped her. But before she could speak, he went on. "It's here we have had our chance," he told her. "Annie and all the rest of us Fosters. This place has been good to us. So in four years, I'll be back. That spring, you'll finish high school."

And so she would. The years would not pass her by, either. They would not leave her where she was now. She wanted to tell him this.

"And I'll be—" She started to say, "eighteen years old," but some way that didn't seem quite the whole truth. "I'll be *close to nineteen years old,*" she finished, as the wonder of the statement swept over her. No doubt about being grown up at nineteen.

"Yes," he said, "I know."

The train was closer now. She could see the smoke, hear the clicking on the rails. Only a few more minutes— only a few—

"Listen to me, Carolyn Pierce," he told her, his face earnest, intent. "We're a new country out here, a pioneer country. We can't stand around and wait for things to happen. We have to go out and get things for ourselves."

"Yes," she said, not seeing what he was driving at, but still realizing it must be something important and right.

"We marry early and we start homes of our own—that's the way it goes in new countries. By the time I come back, some fellow is going to be hanging around you, wanting you to marry him."

"Oh, my goodness!" Carolyn exclaimed, feeling her cheeks grow red at the very thought.

"And don't you do it," he told her. "Do you understand me? *Don't you do it!*"

The train was drawing to a halt now, huffing and puffing away at a great rate. Jim looked at it, then back at Carolyn. He evidently didn't mean to board the train until he had put his idea over to her.

"Don't you do it," he repeated urgently, "because I'm coming back here and marry you myself. Do you hear me? I know now that one of the reasons why this land is good is because you are here."

"Oh, my goodness!" Carolyn said again, scarcely above a whisper.

"All abo-oard!" the conductor called.

Jim hesitated, then turned and ran toward the train, swinging up on the steps just as it started moving. Once there, he turned to face her.

"Remember," he told her. "Remember!"

The train was moving faster now, a plume of smoke rolling back over it like the mane of a wild horse being ridden for the first time. Jim had never ridden on a train before. For him, it was an unbroken horse.

We're a new country out here, a pioneer country. We can't stand around and wait for things to happen.

Jim was a pioneer, in a way, going off into a strange new world.

We marry early—

Across the widening distance, his voice came back to her again. "Remember!" he called.

If she didn't answer him, he might hang out on those steps all the way to Austin. He was going away, and she, too, had a part to play. She put her hands to her lips, making a kind of trumpet out of them. She didn't hesitate at all. She spoke so clearly he had to hear her.

"Yes," she called to him. "Yes—I'll remember."

He heard her. She could tell he had because he put his hand to his mouth and blew her a triumphant kiss.

She moved her own fingers slightly until they, too, had touched her lips. Then she sent a kiss back to him.

All eyes and big words—

"I'll remember—" she said under her breath. "I'll be *'scruciatingly* proud to remember."

LOULA GRACE ERDMAN

is a Missourian by birth and rearing, Texan by adoption. She came directly from the University of Wisconsin to teach, first in the public schools of Amarillo, Texas, later at West Texas State College, in Canyon, where she is now an instructor of creative writing. A different world greeted her in Texas, one so recently established that some of the original settlers were still alive.

She began writing as a hobby. Her first adult novel, *The Years of the Locust,* with a Missouri setting, won the *Dodd, Mead-Redbook Prize.* Her first Texas book, *The Edge of Time,* dealt with the homesteaders of the Texas Panhandle. For this she did a vast amount of research, talking with old timers, haunting the Panhandle Plains Historical Museum, located on the college campus. She came out with box after box of notes, much more than she could use.

These left-over notes formed the basis for *The Wind Blows Free,* a book for young people, winner of the *Dodd, Mead-American Girl Literary Award.* Loula Grace Erdman says of it, "While it was the story of a homesteading family, Melinda, the oldest girl, was supposed to be the heroine. Actually, in the first version, Katie, the second sister, stole the show so that the book had to be revised in order to give Melinda her proper place. It was Dorothy Bryan, Juvenile

Editor of Dodd, Mead, who said Katie must have her own book some day. She continued to say that until finally the book was in her hands!"

After the first two books about the Pierce family, *The Wind Blows Free* and *The Wide Horizon,* were published, Loula Grace Erdman received many letters from young people asking for a third book, with Carolyn as the heroine. The deciding letter came from a young friend, Martha Hughes, whose father is Professor Jack T. Hughes, head of the Geology Department at West Texas State College and Curator of Paleontology at the Panhandle Plains Historical Museum at Canyon, Texas, which has furnished Miss Erdman with much of the background material for her stories set in the Panhandle of Texas. Her mother, Pollyanna Hughes, herself a writer, types the final copies of Miss Erdman's books; her brother David was the model for Ned in the author's adult novel, *The Far Journey.* Martha read the manuscript of *The Good Land* while it was being written. It seems very appropriate that this book is dedicated to Martha.